THIS ORDINARY LIFE

JENNIFER WALKUP

LUMINIS BOOKS

LUMINIS BOOKS
Published by Luminis Books
1950 East Greyhound Pass, #18, PMB 280,
Carmel, Indiana, 46033, U.S.A.
Copyright © Jennifer Walkup, 2015

PUBLISHER'S NOTICE
This is a work of fiction. Names, characters, places, and incidents are either the product of the
author's imagination or are used fictitiously. Any resemblance to actual persons, living or dead,
business establishments, events, or locales is entirely coincidental.

ISBN: 978-1-941311-88-2

Printed in the United States of America

10 9 8 7 6 5 4 3 2 1

For Owen,
My favorite superhero

Early praise for *This Ordinary Life:*

"The relationship between Jasmine and her little brother, Danny, will break your heart and put it back together again."

—Rachael Allen, author of *17 First Kisses* and *The Revenge Playbook*

"This Ordinary Life rises well above the ordinary; while the romance is swoon-worthy, it is the love between Jasmine and her little brother that makes the book so vibrant and harrowingly real."

—Tracy Banghart, author of the *Rebel Wing* series

"I adore *This Ordinary Life*! It has so much heart and soul, it's like I walked into Jasmine's life and left on the last page knowing her. The radio show premise is new and fresh. This book has everything: a main character to root for, a little brother you want to take into your arms and hug, and a romance that's swoon-worthy. If ever there was a boy in a YA book I'd want my own daughter to date, it's Wes!"

—Jaime Blair, author of *Leap of Faith* and *Lost to Me*

Praise for *Second Verse:*

"Deliciously creepy and hauntingly beautiful, *Second Verse* satisfied my urge for both thrills and romance, all in one exciting package. Just be warned: extreme fear of the dark—and barns—might occur as a result of reading."

—Debra Driza, author of *MILA 2.0*

"A supernatural murder mystery with a love interest rooted in the past and present . . . A fast-paced thriller best read with the lights on."

—*Kirkus Reviews*

"A beautifully written story of love and loss that weaves past and present into a haunting tale that will keep you guessing until the final pages."

—Dawn Rae Miller, author of the *Sensitives Trilogy* and *Crushed*

"Part mysterious ghost story and part thriller, *Second Verse's* twists will keep you riveted. The intense connection between Lange and Vaughn is electric. A truly original debut."

—Cindy Pon, author of *Silver Phoenix* and *Fury of the Phoenix*

THIS ORDINARY LIFE

1

THE SHOWER IS no help this morning.

I try all the tricks that normally jump start my thoughts. Long, relaxing shower, really hot water. I wash my hair slowly and condition it twice. I even use the back brush as an impromptu microphone. But even still, the right words don't come.

"Hi, I'm Jasmine Torres, and I am super happy to meet you!"

Super happy? Ugh.

I squirt more body wash into my palm.

"Hey there, Jasmine Torres here. And you are…"

Amateur.

"Hi. I'm Jasmine Torres, radio host at Easton High. I am really glad to be here."

Not bad.

I say it again as I step out of the shower. Wrapping a towel around me, I grab my phone from the counter and type the words into my notes section. Lame? Maybe. But I can read and reread it, and practice on the bus.

Going on this field trip is nothing like being on the air. When I'm on the radio show, words come naturally. Broadcasting is like breathing, really.

But on a day like today, when the Easton High radio show students are going on a field trip, to WYN60, one of the biggest radio stations in New York City? When we'll be talking about doing possible summer internships with them? Well, on days like today, I can hardly string two words together and even with my shower monologue practice, my words and ideas are still all tangled, like tangled worse than my ridiculously curly hair on a windy beach day.

And now I'm running late. Crap. Way to waste time, Jasmine.

I'm twenty minutes behind schedule by the time I dry off. I shoot across the hall to my room, sliding into the carefully chosen and planned outfit for today's trip. It's still school-ish, my absolute favorite shirt, a cute yellow cotton top that ties around the waist, but the black pants make it professional enough to make me look serious and mature.

At least I hope.

I'm dressed in no time, hair scrunched with product and curls somewhat tamed, before I make a mad dash to the kitchen.

On my way through the living room, I tug mom's hair, naturally curly and frizzy like mine. Hopefully it's the only thing I've inherited from her. "Wake up, wake up."

She groans, and nestles further into the couch's threadbare fabric. A scratching noise from the old record player scrapes, the needle turning against nothing. She must have fallen asleep playing old albums again. I roll my eyes. I wish she'd get rid of that stupid thing.

"Not today, Mom. You need to get up now." I shuffle everything in the fridge, hoping we didn't run out of applesauce. There was a decent amount left yesterday, but if someone got in here...

"Mom," I yell. "Get up! You have Danny's IEP meeting at 10:30 and I have to leave, like, now. Get up, get up!"

Score. The glass applesauce container sits behind a mostly empty bottle of wine. I pull it out, grabbing a medicine cup and the collection of meds Danny takes three times a day. The silverware drawer is empty. With a sigh, I pick through the sink of last night's dinner dishes and bottles of mom's apparently one person liquid-only after dinner party.

2

I wash the spoon and grab two plastic syringes, quickly measuring out two of the liquid meds. Caps on, reshelf. Crack open two capsules and empty in the concoction, then finally crush the last pill. Mix it all together and viola, time to wake my brother. I rush down the hall, opening the door with my hip.

"Wake up, Danny," I say in a soft, sing song voice. Waking Danny nicely always bodes well for all our mornings.

"Dan-ny." I snap up the shades. My seven year old brother rolls over and groans, but he smiles at me.

"Jazzy!" he sits up, rubbing his eyes, his hair going in every direction. With his eyes closed, he opens his mouth, like a baby bird, while I spoon the medicine in. Five scoops and done.

"Get yourself ready. I'll leave a bagel on the counter. I gotta run. Make sure she gets up and gets you there."

Danny blinks rapidly. I've given him way too much information before he's barely awake. But I do have to get going. I kiss his head, and run back to my room, slip on shoes and scrunch my fingers in my hair to calm it as much as I can in about two minutes. Makeup takes another three and I'm done. I grab a glass of cold water from the bathroom and dump it on Mom's head as I pass the couch again.

She screams, her voice threatening. "Jasmine, get your ass back here!"

She's on her feet, bleary-eyed from the look of her, but coming through the kitchen. I smile as I close the door behind me. At least she's up.

And me? I've got ten minutes to get to school.

I stop at the end of my driveway, where the weeds reach almost to my knees around our mailbox. The driveway is empty. The street too. Sebastian is nowhere to be found, though he should have been here to pick me up at least ten minutes ago. I blow breath into my bangs, fanning myself in the already too-warm morning.

Come on Sebastian. Of all days to be late?

I have three options. Hoof it all the way across town to school—not optimal as it will take way too long and I'll be sweating like crazy and frantic by the time I get there. Or, I could go back in my house and attempt to make my no doubt pissed off mom actually drive me to school. I take a step toward the back door, actually considering it, but no amount of begging would convince her after that water stunt I pulled. I look at the faded blue paint of our small house, and the flower beds overgrown with years' of weeds and ivy. I sigh. Getting her to cooperate is as hopeless as this place.

Last option? I can make the five block trek to Sebastian's and hope he just overslept and is still there.

I hike my backpack up on my shoulders and turn toward Sebastian's, shaking my head as I kick a rock that's in my way as I rush down the street. My boyfriend is late at least ninety percent of the time. He's lucky I like him as much as I do.

The sun presses on me like a heavy blanket as I rush down the block. I quickly pull my hair up, tying it loosely enough so it won't leave a ponytail mark. I've been an alternate radio personality for Easton High's station since I was a freshman. And with today's trip, our radio crew is not only going to the station and learning about the internships (internships!), but will also be observing WYN60's Get Up and Go show as well as the changeover to their afternoon team. If I miss this trip... I can't. It's WYN60. In New York City. The Get Up and Go show! Just being in that building will be a dream come true. And if I actually do get a chance at that internship it will mean a much bigger hope when it comes time for college applications, maybe even scoring some much needed scholarship money if I can prove myself.

I move quickly beneath the unseasonably hot sun, wiping a layer of sweat off the back of my neck, my favorite bangle bracelets clanking against each other on my wrist. I fan my face and curse Sebastian under my breath. Why couldn't he have just been on time?

But when I turn onto his block, the anger falls away. Seeing him will calm my nerves and help me deal with the pressure of today. The thought of his smile and newly cropped hair makes my stomach swirl. I imagine him coming out of his house, fresh out of the shower, smelling like shampoo and aftershave and pulling me against his chest into one of his awesome, tight hugs. He always kisses the top of my head, then my forehead, before moving on to my lips. I have to admit, it's a routine I've enjoyed over the last eleven months.

Sebastian is an unorganized mess and can be a real pain in my butt, but he is always there for me. My family is chock full of issues, and honestly, without my BFF Frankie and Sebastian to constantly listen to me and be there to pick up the pieces when things fall apart? Not sure how I'd deal with it.

There's only five blocks between my house and Sebastian's but it feels like another world. My neighborhood isn't rough, exactly, we have grass in the yard and we have driveways, but we don't have two story homes and neat curbs and sprawling porches like this street. Sebastian's house sits at the end of the cul-de-sac. His car, a Range Rover—but used, so less obnoxious (eye roll)—is still in his driveway. I huff.

I skip around to the side of the house, buoyed by the idea of seeing him. Life sucks sometimes, but when Sebastian pulls me into that warm hug, the whole stress of the morning will melt away faster than a Popsicle in summer.

The gate is propped open. I frown, hoping Misha didn't get out. The Pomeranian is a four year old princess of a dog and if the gate is ever left open, we get an earful from Seb's mom. I mean, she loves that dog almost as much as she loves Sebastian and his brothers—which is to say, they're all spoiled as anything, including the dog. And since Sebastian's older brothers are away at college, she's gotten even worse about catering to her youngest son and the adorable little hairball.

I pull the gate closed. The pool glistens in the morning sun and silence envelopes the huge yard. Not even a bird flaps in the marble birdbath. I stare for a minute too long, remembering that night, last summer, the first time Seb and I went swimming in the pool alone. My eyes flick to the hot tub, remembering his lips on mine that night. I shiver despite the heat. Man, he can push my buttons, even when he's not around. With a huge smile, I walk toward the lower back door—Sebastian's private entrance. Like I said, he's hugely spoiled, and practically has his own apartment on the basement level. The sliding glass door is open slightly, the sheer curtains sucking in and out of the space with the breeze.

Odd. I step through the opening carefully. The living room area is a mess. Cups on the table, pillows on the floor. Okay, this is weird. Sebastian is a bona fide neat freak, as in doesn't even let me drink a soda on his leather couch. There is no way he would ever leave his place like this.

"Hello?" I call out, walking toward the bedroom. A rustling stops me in my tracks. A slamming door beyond the bedroom. What the hell? Did someone break in here? Are they still here? I fumble for my phone. Should I call someone?

"Ohmygod, Seb, you are too much."

The voice is syrupy sweet. Teasing.

Female.

Before I even think about it, I stalk across his living room, through the small kitchenette and open the door so hard I half expect it to come off its hinges. I'm greeted by my boyfriend's bare back as he leans over his bed, jeans so low on his waist that the gray band of his underwear stands out against his olive skin.

6

Beneath him, skinny fake-tan legs poke out, a mini skirt riding up to practically expose her underwear.

My phone vibrates in my hand. I glance at it quickly, barely able to tear my eyes off my soon to be ex-boyfriend. I push it to silent. Why does my mom choose now to call?

"So I guess this explains why you're always late!"

Sebastian jumps up so fast it's like he's been shot by a slingshot.

"Jazz! It's not what you think," he says, having the nerve to stand there half naked with some girl looking alternately bugeyed terrified of me, and yet still reaching her hand out toward his.

Tears burn behind my eyes like fire, but I will not cry. My phone buzzes again and once again I click it to silent mode.

"Whatever," I say smoothly, trying so hard to keep my voice even. "I'm sure you and your, um, friend will get to school whenever you're done here." I nod toward the girl on the bed, who has at least had the decency to pull the sheet over her legs. Her face is bright red and she looks like she could die from embarrassment. If only.

My phone buzzes again and I shove it into my back pocket and turn to leave.

"Jazz wait."

I take a deep breath, looking into the kitchen. Having my back to them helps the storm raging inside me settle but Sebastian's deep voice tries to weasel its way into that place in my heart that is his. Screw that. None of me is his.

I turn back to him, the flame inside igniting as if doused with gasoline.

"I wait for no one, Sebastian, not even you." And I turn on my heel for real this time, making my way out of the room. The tears threaten to dump out of me. I have to get out of here. He follows me through the living room.

"You can't go."

I spin around. "Really? And what would you propose if I stay here? We sit down and have a chat with *her?*"

"It's not like that."

I cock my head, wondering what in God's name he could possibly come up with to explain this. No one is that smooth. "Red freaking handed, Seb. Red freaking handed. How could you do this?" I choke on a sob, my traitor tears leaking from the corners of my eyes.

Sebastian looks over his shoulder and then back at me. "Just give me a minute," he whispers. "We can talk this out."

"Whispering? Are you freaking whispering? As if *I'm* the other woman?" I shake my head, disgusted. And then a thought slaps me across the face. "*Am* I the other woman?"

"Of course not, listen."

"No need." I wave him off. "I am done. D. O. N. E. Done with you."

The wall phone rings. After four rings, it stops. Sebastian just stares at me. I don't let myself get pulled into the dark sea of his eyes. I can't.

The phone starts to ring again. "Do you need to get that? Maybe it's the girl behind door number three?"

My cell rings again and I whip it from my pocket. Mom again. Jesus, her timing is horrendous.

"What?" I practically scream into the phone. "I'm in the middle of something, can you stop calling? Sorry about the water thing this morning, but this isn't—"

"I've been trying you everywhere." She's breathless, her voice an empty shell of itself. Not like Mom at all.

My stomach drops like a sack of flour, heavy and splitting open.

"It's Danny," she says. "Ambulance is on the way. It's… bad. I don't know. You're usually here and, I wasn't sure what to do… what I was supposed to do."

"I'll be there in two seconds." I click the call off and rush for the door.

"I'll drive you." Sebastian says, already beside me, keys jingling in hand. I nod. The last thing I want is for him to do anything for me. But I have to get home to my family. I have to get to my brother as fast as I can.

2

THE AMBULANCE, TWO police cars and an EMT truck are already at the curb when Sebastian turns onto my street. I open the door and jump out before the car is fully stopped.

"Jazz, do you want me to—"

"Just go." I wave a hand at him. I dart across my lawn as if shot from a cannon. My hands shake as I push the back door open. It's chaos incarnate in my living room with uniforms all over the place and police radios beeping and spitting walky talkie voices.

I rush to Danny, settling into the only small space available, at his feet. He lies on his side, eyes closed. Beside him, the EMTs take his vitals, blood pressure cuff on his right arm. Beneath the plastic oxygen mask, his small lips are nearly purple and stuck in a pursed position as if to give a goodnight kiss.

I pull his hand into mine. He's totally limp.

"How long?" I say bending to kiss his little fingers. His skin is still baby soft.

Mom stands behind the couch huddled with two police officers. Tears stream down her cheeks, dragging streaks of last night's eyeliner with them. Anger flares in me, wondering if she even saw the seizure start or if she was busy doing her own thing.

"I'm, I'm not sure," she says. "When I walked into his room, he was flopped on the floor in a weird way…"

God. Just as I expected. I jump up. "Well how long before that did you see or talk to him?"

She blinks rapidly. "I'm not sure. I mean, he was getting ready. I called out to him."

"You went back to sleep, didn't you? You didn't see or talk to him before this. Did you?" My tone is lethal and the police officers step toward me.

"Jasmine, I was getting ready. For the meeting, at his school."

I look behind her into the kitchen. The bagel I made for Danny still sits on the counter.

"He never came out of his room?" I ask incredulously. Nothing could keep carb-loving Danny from his bagel. "I left what… God, half an hour ago? Was he out of it that long?"

I sink down to my knees. If Danny had been seizing that long… this could be really bad. Behind me, the EMT lays Danny on the stretcher.

"Mom. Did. You. See. Him. At. All. After I left? *Do not lie*." I practically growl the last words.

Tears spill down her cheeks again and she shakes her head, her thin shoulders trembling. "No," she whispers. "I didn't."

I rush to Danny's side as they wheel him out of the house.

"Only one person can come along," the EMT says, looking at Mom.

She nods. "Let Jasmine go. I'll follow in my car." She looks down at her hands. "Jazz can answer more questions about his medicine and stuff anyway. She usually takes care of all that for me."

The female officer looks between us and nods. She gives me a sympathetic smile.

"Come on then." The EMT motions for me to get outside and into the ambulance. "He seems stable now, but we have to get him hooked up to see what's going on."

11

Forget school today. Forget WYN60. Forget everything. I hop into the back of the ambulance, holding Danny's hand as we pull away from the curb. It's amazing that only this morning I was completely excited about that dumb trip and possible internship. Not to mention blindsided by Sebastian and whoever she was.

I'd give up every school trip, every internship, every chance at any scholarship even, and every chance at having a boyfriend who cared about me—Sebastian or otherwise. I'd give up everything.

I will, actually, I promise God or whatever entity out there may be listening. *I'd sell my soul if it meant my little brother would never have another seizure again.*

THE HOSPITAL VISIT is like all the others. Danny wakes up as we're getting settled. He looks around, disoriented and sleepy faced, like he did when he was four and all this was just starting.

"Shhh," I say, smoothing back his sweaty hair. "We're at the hospital. Just going to do some tests."

The technician comes into the room a few minutes later. I hit play on the room's DVD player and sit back while she starts to apply the EEG monitoring pads to Danny's head. He holds my hand tightly as he watches one of the newer Disney movies I haven't seen. I drop my head back and close my eyes, listening to the hiss and hum of the technician's machine—shooting air to dry the glue on each pad she applies. That and the Disney music lulls me into a state of near sleep as I wait for mom and the others.

Two hours later we've been set up in Danny's room—a nice room down in the new pediatric wing. Mom sits on one side of him and me at the foot of his bed, Danny eating chicken fingers and fries while watching television. Other than the pack of wires attached to his head and the IV in his arm, he looks content, like he's having a great time, even. No school, snacks, lots of television. For him, this is practically a vacation.

Mom yawns in this totally exaggerated way, stretching her hands up and back as if she's in an aerobics class or something.

Drama much? I fight the urge to roll my eyes.

My gaze flicks to the daisy chain tattoo that circles her wrist. I ignore the vice that tightens my already knotted-up stomach. Childhood memories, especially good ones, tend to tie my emotions up worse than anything.

"I'm going to head down to Starbucks and get some coffee," she says. "You want some?"

"Sure. Just black is fine. Grab a few sugar packets." I don't take my eyes off Danny. He doesn't have seizures that often anymore, but when he does, they can often set off a chain reaction where he will have more throughout the day. I study his features, watching for any twitch, flicker or flinch that something may be wrong. Mom stands there for another minute, looking up at the television. When she finally leaves, I let out a relaxing breath.

I don't want to feel this angry around her all the time, but what choice do I have? I mean, look what happened this morning. She's not the mom she used to be. And I'm certainly not the little girl I was either, the one without heaps of responsibilities, who used to pick daisies with her happy mom and make chains for our hair and wrists. I even kept a box of them for so long. I remember crying when they accidentally got thrown out. Wow. I wish that was my biggest problem now.

My vision blurs and I wipe the tears away, pulling my chair a little closer to my brother's bed.

"Danny?" I say. Staring at the TV, he doesn't answer. My heart leaps in my chest and I jump up and rush to the side of his bed.

Danny turns to me with a confused expression. "What's up?"

Thank God.

Relax, Jasmine. Not every single nuance is a seizure.

"Oh," I say, trying to cover up my paranoia with a tight smile. "Want to do something? I can go down and get checkers from the game room?"

"Yes!" he says. "And Connect Four? How about chess? You said you were gonna teach me chess."

I smooth a hand carefully over the collection of nodes and wires on his head. He looks up at me with his big brown eyes, long eyelashes blinking against his pale cheeks. I swallow the bulging lump of emotion in my throat and nod.

"Whatever you want," I say. "I'll go see what they have. Unless you'd rather do homework? I think Mom brought your backpack."

"What!" He wrinkles his nose in disgust.

"I'm kidding," I say, laughing. "You get a day off school, let's make it a day off school."

Danny yawns widely and nestles further into his pillow. "I'm tired, Jazzy."

"Tell you what," I say, moving the tray of food away. "Go ahead and take a nap, and I'll see what I can find down in the game room for when you wake up."

I walk to the window to adjust the blinds. Darkness fills the room, as if it's some quiet, pre-dawn hour instead of mid-afternoon. I kiss my brother's forehead. The pungent smell of adhesive glue from the electrodes on his head stings my nose.

"Sweet dreams," I say.

He has a roommate, from the looks of the rumpled sheets and duffle bag on the next bed. I frown. Private rooms are best, but this is a big and busy hospital. It's not always possible to get one. I hope whoever owns the navy blue backpack with the LIFE IS GOOD and LIFE IS BETTER IN AN AIRPLANE patches sown on

14

is quiet enough and doesn't have a hugely loud family. Danny needs his rest and to stay calm to get accurate test results.

I sigh and stare toward the hallway, thinking about the WYN60 trip I'm missing right now. I blink a few times to clear the tears until everything comes into focus.

I imagine them, watching Get Up and Go broadcast. I can see it now, the morning show team around a table, inviting the field trip students to come hang out with them and check out the equipment and broadcast area. My imagination lands on detail after detail, the headphones and microphones, the scrolling news and celebrity gossip on monitors on the table. I imagine cups of coffee, a huge spread of half-eaten breakfast—bagels and croissants and muffins, and the smiles of the radio show as they meet Ms. Hudson and the kids on the trip.

Smiles to everyone but me.

I let out a shuddering breath and look at my brother. I watch his skinny chest rise and fall with sleep, wires falling all around his face from beneath the mesh cap on his head. How can I even think about the trip and wish I was there? This is more important.

I push away the bitter disappointment and settle back into my chair using the small bit of light from the TV to read my chemistry textbook. Boring, but I am totally behind. Mr. Karns takes no prisoners and we have a test next week.

My mind drifts to the trip again. I'll talk to Ms. Hudson. Maybe I can still apply for the internship, even without meeting the crew. I sigh, shutting my chem book and look at the monitor next to Danny. No matter how many times we've been through this, I never know what any of the squiggly lines and brain waves mean. My eyes dart across the screen, imagining it shows that every single brain wave is doing exactly what it should be, that this test will show that Danny is all better. But I don't need to be a literal brain surgeon to know that isn't the case.

My phone buzzes and my best friend's name lights up the screen. I texted her the basic details of the morning when we got here but haven't updated her yet.

"Hey," I whisper. "I can't really talk."

"Me neither," Frankie says. "I got a bathroom pass to sneak a call to you. I wanted to make sure you're okay. How's Danny?" Hearing my best friend's voice brings tears to the surface. What I would give to have her sitting here with me.

"So-so, don't really know anything yet."

"I wish I could help," she says. "Is there anything I can do?"

I sniff. "Thanks, but not really. I'll text when I know anything."

"Okay. So. What the hell with Sebastian? Your text was shocking."

My stomach drops. "Yeah well. He's an asshole. Shocking is definitely the word for what I saw."

"You actually, physically caught him?"

"Oh yeah. In all his glory. Half naked with some girl in his bed."

"I can't believe it."

"Me neither. I mean, how the hell could he do this?"

"Do you know who she was?"

"Not a clue. She was vaguely familiar. I can't even think about it right now." Though how could I not? I mean, the image is permanently burned in my retinas. How could the guy who I thought was my everything treat me like I'm nothing?

Frankie pauses, but I can tell it's a meaningful one.

"What aren't you telling me?" I ask.

"Well... I just wanted to tell you before you come back, people are talking about it."

"How does anyone even know?"

Another pause.

"He changed his relationship status to single online."

16

It's like I've been punched in the gut. I slump in the chair and pinch the bridge of my nose.

"He what? I can't even process this. What?"

"I'm sorry," Frankie says quietly. "I didn't want to bug you with this when you're there, but I figured if you saw it, or if someone texted or emailed… I wanted you to hear it from me instead. I'm sorry. I didn't mean to make it worse."

"No. You didn't make it worse. I don't understand. After everything that happened, and the way it happened. Wow. He was certainly in a rush to let the world know he's available I guess." My voice goes hard but Frankie knows me better than that.

"I love you," she says. "He doesn't deserve you anyway. I'll keep an eye out for gossip, but just be with your family now. Text me later?"

"Yeah, okay. Thanks."

"Besties?"

"Forever." I answer with the second half of our standard goodbye.

When we hang up, I turn my phone off and throw it in my bag. I can't believe I thought I loved him. Just the thought of it turns my stomach inside out.

Danny snores quietly on his bed and I watch his little chest rise and fall through my tear-blurred vision.

I stand and stretch, wondering where mom went for the coffee. Maybe I can rustle up some subpar coffee in the hall lounge here. I mute the TV and step away from Danny, my arms wrapped around my middle as if I can hold all the broken pieces of myself together.

"Be right back," I whisper to my sleeping brother. I push all other thoughts from my mind. Frankie is right. I need to focus on my family now, on Danny.

On my way out, I notice a stack of comics on the other bed in Danny's room. Great. It's going to be some loud little kid who watches Batman or whatever all day. Bam Pow Wham. I can hear it now.

I decide to take a stroll past the nurses' station on my way to the crappy coffee room. My shoes squeak on the tiles and I keep my gaze on the floor, playing a game with myself as I walk down the hall, stepping only on the used-to-be-white-when-they-were-new tiles, and not on the alternating pastels. I'm hopeful as I reach the end of the hall. If any of our favorite nurses are on call, maybe I can sweet talk them into moving Danny to a private room.

No such luck. I barely recognize any of the three women at the desk. Maybe it's been longer than I realized since we were frequent flyers here at the illustrious St. Bonaventure pediatric neurological ward. Not a bad thing. The nurses, all clad in cheerful scrubs, return my tired smile with exhausted ones of their own.

I wait for the coffee in the automatic machine. It gurgles and hisses behind me while I read the announcements on the bulletin board, all printed on super colorful paper about various activities, crafts, and entertainment that will be happening all week. The hospital really tries to cheer the kids up and keep them busy. Tomorrow, a neon pink page tells me, Lucky the Black Lab therapy dog will be visiting, as well as Junior the clown. On a bright yellow sheet I see that today the Musictime Live for Kids will be making rounds right before the story time, bingo, and make your own loom bracelet hours.

Reading the notices dredges up the worst memories of some of Danny's early and very long visits. I think about how drugged they had him, how he hardly woke for days and when he did, how he could barely walk. So small and so sedated. It was the only way to stop his seizures back then.

The days he was awake he did many of these same activities pegged all over this bulletin board. Playing instruments with the music group, shaking maracas and tambourines; his eyes lighting up, despite the drugged sheen in them, when the magician made a rainbow scarf appear out of his ear.

Walking down the short hall, Mom or I trailing his IV pole behind him, would exhaust him. How Mom was so much more present then. Sure, the drinking had already started at home, but it hadn't invaded every bit of her yet. Here with the doctors, she used to ask all the right questions. Take notes on what they said, even.

It feels like a lifetime ago.

I picture her this morning, all ratty hair and last night's makeup. Smelling like she'd spilled more than one drink on herself. Hungover Mom.

Everything always changes.

My traitorous, overtired mind is apparently intent on making me suffer by snowballing through all the good memories, all the freaking used-to-bes. Like right now, it causes physical pain to my insides, as if my internal organs are pin cushions in maximum capacity use, to remember how Sebastian—at one point a new and good boyfriend—spent day after day here with me during some of Danny's longer hospital stays.

And now he's *status: single.*

Whatever. I close my eyes, instantly seeing this morning's scene in my mind. Who was she? She of the mini skirt in my boyfriend's bed? How could he? God, how freaking could he? I respect myself way too much to even talk to him again, let alone ask him about it, but it's going to kill me to not know the details. How long was it going on? Was everything between us a lie?

Thankfully a ding on the coffee machine alerts me to my Fresh When You Want It! cup of coffee. I grab it and head back toward Danny's room.

I walk quietly past the mostly open doors. A baby cries down at the other end of the hall, but it's pretty quiet over here. When I turn the corner, a woman walks out of our room. She's tall, with long curly hair held back by movie star sunglasses. Her bag slips from her shoulder, and crashes to the floor, spilling half its contents around her feet. She bends to pick it up and her sunglasses slide off her head.

"Can I help?" I squat down to help her push random purse things into her bag—lip gloss, wallet, tampons—and she gives me a million-watt smile.

"Thanks, Darlin'," she says with a southern drawl. I look behind her, wondering what this stranger was doing in Danny's room. Her smile grows wide, deepening the harsh laugh lines and crow's feet that, even still, can't hide her beauty.

"I'm Lynette," she says as we straighten up. "My son is in this room."

What? Her son? "Oh! He must be my brother's roommate. My brother is Danny. He was sleeping when I left. I better go check on him."

"All's quiet as a church mouse in there. Wesley is just readin' anyway. I told him to keep down his TV and music too while that little boy is sleepin'. You'd think they'd be all private rooms by now, but no." She blows a puff of breath into her bangs. "Anyway, I'll be back in a bit. I'll see you soon."

"Um, sure. Yeah. See you soon."

"What's your name, honey?"

"Jasmine. I'm Jasmine." I shake the hand she has outstretched and nod toward the room. "Well, I better get back."

"Of course, see you around." And with that, Lynette turns on her heel and sashays down the hall in a cloud of flowery perfume.

I peek into my room, hoping Danny is still resting. The chairs at the foot of his bed are still unoccupied. Where did Mom go for that coffee? Pennsylvania? Good thing they don't have a bar in the hospital. I snort at my own joke, not even because it's funny, but because I'm too exhausted to think past the sad reality that she probably really would do something like that if she could.

I walk quietly into the room, eyes darting to the bed next to Danny's to see who Lynette's superhero-loving son is. I brace myself for the inevitable little kid onslaught of questions. For some reason, kids gravitate to me like I'm a camp counselor or kindergarten teacher or something.

But the boy lying on the bed next to Danny's is a teenager. A relatively *cute* teenager, too, I notice, though I only get a side eye view as I cross the room. He looks up from something he's reading, probably one of those comic books, I bet, and shakes his head to throw shaggy, dirty-blond hair out of his eyes. His gaze locks on me.

I don't want to be rude, so I give a small wave. "Hi," I whisper.

His head tilts slightly as he considers me. He gives a hello nod back and our eyes meet for just a second. There's a sense of humor in his, but he drops them back to his book quickly, which, I see now, isn't a comic, but a thick text book. I slip into the chair at the foot of Danny's bed and take a big sip of my coffee. Scalding liquid scorches my mouth and I jump in my seat and spill even more of the steaming coffee all over me.

"Damn it," I mutter, wiping the burning liquid from my chin. I pull my wet shirt away from my skin, wincing at the heat. I toss the offending Styrofoam cup of too-hot-and-gross-besides coffee into the trash. A few droplets splash up and hit my hand, burning me again.

Comic book boy chuckles and I look over at his bed, but his eyes are still on his book, his face serious as anything.

I narrow my eyes. Did I imagine that? He better not be laughing at me.

His lip twitches, just slightly, but it's enough for me to see. I stand abruptly and pull the curtain between the beds closed with so much force I'm surprised it doesn't come off the track.

"My brother needs to sleep," I hiss.

I search my bag for napkins and frown at the coffee stains on my shirt, keeping one ear turned toward comic boy's side of the room. He doesn't say anything else, thankfully.

After a few minutes, I feel a little bad. I mean, the guy is obviously in the hospital and I hope he's okay. But still, if there's one thing I hate, it's being laughed at. Especially after the utterly craptastic day I'm having. I plop back into my chair and roll my eyes to the ceiling.

Come on universe, make something good happen.

3

DANNY IS SET to leave the next day. The tech removes the cap and wires and I wash the glue out of his hair. We're both exhausted and badly in need of showers. I stand by the window in Danny's room while he colors and we wait for mom to sign his paperwork and pick us up.

"Want me to make you an Iron Man one?" Danny nods to the coloring book.

"Of course. Make a good one. I'll hang it up at home."

With his tongue caught between his teeth, he frowns in concentration at the page he colors.

"I'm still confused about the knights," he says, still coloring. "I get the other pieces, but why does the knight move that way?"

We'd been over this about a billion times since I attempted to teach him chess in a marathon session last night.

"You just have to practice and get used to it. All the pieces have their own way to move."

"No, I *know* that." He looks up at me and rolls his eyes. "But the knight is *confusing*."

"We have a set at home. We'll play tonight, okay? We'll practice some more."

This seems to satisfy him enough to go back to his coloring, and I look up at the clock. School is probably out for me today, but I'd like to at least try to call Ms. Hudson to see if I can salvage any hope for the Get Up and Go internship.

Fat chance.

At least I get another day without seeing Sebastian. Him and whoever that girl was. Who knows how far the gossip has spread. Another day out of school and maybe it'll be old news by the time I get back.

I bend to touch my toes, trying to stretch out the ache of sleeping in the hospital recliner-bed thing. It's cracked leather and stiff, even if it does open pretty far and they do provide sheets and pillows. And anyway, it was only one night this time.

Mom got called into work last night. She works as a bartender, not coincidentally, I'm sure, and works tons of late nights, as well as some afternoons. On one hand, I know it seems way messed up of her to leave the hospital when Danny was doing an overnight, but on the other, even I have to admit, we need the money and she does make decent cash in tips. And Danny was stable, not a single seizure after that one at home. Plus, I'm here for him.

"I'm gonna go get a drink, Danny. Be right back?"

My brother smiles widely at me and nods. My stomach squeezes on itself. He's such a sweet kid. What did he ever do to deserve this? To get stuck with a crappy mom, a dad who left when he was only a baby, and seizures on top of it? Poor kid. I pull open the curtain separating the beds. Looks like comic book boy is still sleeping, so I move quietly through his side of the room and into the hallway. I decide to forego the crappy coffee and grab a soda from the family fridge instead. Caffeine is caffeine, right?

I stand in the hallway, drinking my soda and watching the banks of elevators. Thanks to my early birthday, a few more months and I'll be eighteen. Then I'll be able to sign Danny in and out as needed. Waiting for Mom is always ridiculously long. She is the Queen of oversleeping and running late.

Whatever. I better get back. I slip quietly into our room.

"Hey Sunny."

My head whips to comic boy, sitting up in bed with a (I have to admit, though it pains me all the way down to my glittery painted toenails) cute smirk on his face. A handful of freckles dust his cheeks, which lift as his smile widens. His front tooth is the slightest bit crooked, I notice, but it gives his smile character. He's definitely cute.

"Excuse me?" I cross my arms, careful not to spill yet another drink and embarrass myself again.

He casually tosses a paper airplane up in the air and catches it again. "That shirt," he says. "I noticed it yesterday. Sunshine. Sunny. Cheerful. In a place like this, it's kind of nice." He winces when he says the words and I soften, hoping he's not in some kind of pain.

"Um," I say. "Are you okay? I mean, God, that was rude. I'm not, like, asking why you're here or whatever. I just noticed you made a face so I thought maybe you were hurting or something. Forget I asked. Sorry."

Oh my God Jasmine, can you stop talking now?

But comic book boy laughs. "No, nothing hurts. I'm good. Was just wincing at my sort of awful line there about your yellow shirt being nice. I mean, what self-respecting guy says that? And I can't even blame it on good drugs, because they didn't give me any this time."

This time. He must be a frequent flyer too.

"Anyway," he says. "If you can forgive my complete lack of coolness in conversation starters, I think we got off on the wrong foot yesterday when you slammed the curtain on me." He shakes his head, mock serious. "I'm not always great with girls but I don't usually get that kind of treatment when I'm in a hospital bed."

My ears burn. "Sorry," I say. "Bad day."

The sarcastic look leaves him as his eyes slide to Danny's side of the room, where my brother still colors, deep in concentration. "Yeah, of course. I'm sorry. I didn't mean to be insensitive. Once again, my jokes fall on the dumb side instead of funny."

"It's fine," I say, noticing how the blue of his eyes is almost precisely the color of the absolute best summer beach sky.

"Anyway, I'm Wes." He holds out a hand for me to shake and I walk to the side of his bed.

"Jasmine."

"Well Jasmine, it's nice to meet you. Though if it's okay, I prefer to call you Sunny."

O-kay. Considering I'll talk to him for all of a few more minutes, he can call me whatever.

His skin is really warm and dry and his fingers grip mine a second longer than they need to.

"Also, good to see you're sticking with cold, non-burning drinks today." His eyes dance with mischief.

I roll mine and finally pull my hand away. He looks healthy enough and there is no sign around here of what's going on. I'm actually considering how to ask when he opens his mouth.

"I know what you're thinking. Why is this perfect specimen of a guy holed up here at St. Bonaventure Pediatric ward?"

"No, I wasn't. I was just going to say—"

But of course my mother chooses that moment to rush in.

"Jasmine!" she practically yells, all out of breath. "I'm double parked! Is Danny signed out?"

I turn where I am, still next to Wes's bed. "Um, no. He needs a parent or guardian to sign him out. Hang on. I'll go tell the nurse." I slip from beside Wes's bed, turning back to give him another small wave as I make my way from the room. He winks at me, but it's not as cheesy as you'd expect a wink to be. It's conspiratorial. Like we're sharing a secret or something. Which makes no sense, I know.

I really need to get some more sleep. My brain is playing tricks on me.

4

I'M UP FOR school the next day with plenty of time to spare. I'm obviously not getting a ride from Sebastian anymore, so I'll be walking most days. On the days Frankie has a car, I'll have a ride, but otherwise, I'll be getting my daily exercise bright and early. I text her to see if she's driving today.

I apply my eyeliner slowly, thinking about how much time I wasted on him. I'm not going to lie, it hurts like hell. He's not only a liar and a cheater but he was in such a rush to tell the world how free and available he is the second we broke up. But whatever, there is no way I'm disrespecting myself enough to chase after him, or even think about taking him back. It's over. My stomach clenches on itself like I'm in the middle of one of those show-up-to-school-naked dreams, but I let out a breath and smooth my eyebrows with my eyebrow brush. I may be shattered inside, but Sebastian will never know.

Besides, Danny is out of the hospital and he seemed perfectly healthy for the rest of the day yesterday, and today I will talk to Ms. Hudson about somehow, some way, getting over to the Get Up and Go show, even though I missed the trip. I need that internship. There is no way I'm getting anywhere near affording college if I don't have some better communications and radio experience to my name. I need that job.

After giving Danny his medicine and setting out his breakfast, I pour a bowl of cereal for myself. I eat it at the counter, scrolling through my phone and hoping Frankie texts me back.

"Jasmine? Why are you up?" Mom asks from behind me. I didn't even hear her come in.

"Uh, school?"

She blinks rapidly and pulls her hair into a messy knot on the top of her head. Her eyes skate to the calendar on the wall, which is two months behind. She turns her red-rimmed eyes back to me. "School?"

"Yeah, the place we go five days a week?"

"I think I need coffee," she says. She shuffles across the kitchen in her too-big sweatpants. "That whole hospital stay really threw me off this week. I swore today was Saturday."

I snort. "I wish. It's Wednesday, Mom."

She chugs half a cup of black coffee. How she doesn't burn her throat, I don't know.

I rinse my bowl in the sink. "Danny had his meds. His bagel is on the table."

Mom steps closer and puts a clammy hand on my face. She smells like sweat and vodka. "Thanks, sweetie. I appreciate your help. Things will get easier for us around here. Thanks for pitching in so much."

"No problem," I grumble, reaching down to pick up my bag. "You working tonight?"

"It's Wednesday? Yes. I'm working the late shift. That okay for you to be here for Danny?"

"Yeah, of course. Is there any food?"

"There's leftovers," she says, sipping her coffee. "And tonight is Amir's night in the kitchen. That means I'll bring lots of stuff home."

My stomach rumbles. The bar where Mom works has a pretty good kitchen. When Amir, her favorite chef, is cooking, he always makes us extra. It'll keep us well fed for a few days, at least.

"Nice," I answer. "Hopefully it's prime rib sandwich night."

"Not asparagus night?" She jokes.

28

"God no!" I grimace and Mom laughs at the depth of my hatred for the vegetable.

"Anyway, I gotta run." I hike my backpack up on my back.

"Have a good day," Mom answers while she fills her coffee mug again.

SINCE FRANKIE NEVER answered my text, I start walking. With all my thoughts spiraling in every direction, the walk to school goes faster than I remember it used to. I'm only a few blocks away, walking in the shade of the huge and gorgeous elms on Park Street, when Frankie's green Jetta pulls up next to me, windows down.

"So sorry! I was running late and didn't get your text!" She yells across the passenger seat, looking at me over the dark sunglasses she's let slip down her nose.

"No worries," I say as I pull the door open. I plop into my seat and turn to my best friend, anxiety coiling through me. "Tell me everything. Are the rumors as bad as I think they are?"

Frankie slams the car into drive and speeds away from the curb, her dark, perfectly straightened hair blowing toward her open sunroof. "Who cares about that crap? I already told you Sebastian is playing the victim." She rolls her eyes.

"Yeah, but I want details. I need to know exactly what I'm getting myself into."

Frankie huffs and makes a right turn instead of the left that takes us to school.

"Uh, Frankie?"

"Coffee first," she says, pursing her bubblegum pink lips. "Always, coffee first."

I stare at her, waiting for her to start talking, but she looks straight ahead, her eye on the prize. Frankie is nothing if not serious about coffee. I lean forward and turn on her radio, flipping it to AM.

"Who's broadcasting this morning?" she says, eying the digital numbers that flash across the screen.

"Probably Romeo or Justine." I shrug. I'm one of the only serious radio students at Easton this year, and even though there are a few others who host the morning and afternoon radio shows, most of them are into the production side of things. Or signed up just to look good on college applications. "Who cares. I'm more interested in what Big Dee is playing these days."

Frankie turns to me, eyebrows raised. She smacks my hand away and turns the radio off. "Are you crazy? Are you not tortured enough this morning?"

"Fine. But there's nothing wrong with seeing what the competition is up to." I sit back against the seat and look out the window. And it's true. Chester High, only a few towns over, is the only nearby school with a decent radio station. And DJ Big Dee, as she goes by, though she's nothing more than a tiny little thing, is pretty much the only other decent high school DJ around. Last year they had a local spin-off contest for high school DJs at the Bentley County holiday bazaar, and she and I were the two finalists. Even after three additional sets each, it was declared a tie. I don't listen to her show often, but I'm not stupid. I'm sure she's applying for the WYN60 internship too. I'm also not stupid enough that I think she's my only competition. I'm sure DJs from all over are applying for the high school internship spot. I may need it more than them, but if I have to lose, it better not be to her. Of course that's *if* I even have a chance of going for it at this point.

Anyway. First things first.

"Come on," I say. "Give me the details on the Sebastian situation. It's like, your top duty as my best friend."

"Shhh." She pulls into a parking spot and nods to the coffee shop. "Coffee first."

Once we have our iced coffees she turns to me in the parking lot. "It's messy," she says. "But overall you don't have to worry, I think, because people probably like you more than they like him."

"*Like* me more? Debatable. I barely talk to anyone besides you. And anyway, this isn't a popularity contest."

Frankie starts driving again. "Sebastian's a cocky ass and you're one of the school DJs. You do the math."

I sigh.

"So whatever. He's playing the victim. You guys have been together for like two million years."

"Eleven months."

"Same thing. You seemed perfect and now you're broken up. So he's all *Jasmine dumped me my heart is broken blah blah blah*. Girls were flocked around him at lunch, concerned faces all sad while they listened to him."

"Great. So I'm the bad guy."

"Hardly. I bet everyone can see through his crap."

"Well those girls couldn't."

"Let him be their problem, then."

"True." I drop my head back against the seat. "I don't suppose he told anyone of his extracurricular activities involving girls on the side, did he?"

Frankie snorts. "Of course not. He's nothing but a knight in shining armor, you know. But the rumors of him cheating on you are already running rampant."

I don't know if that makes me feel better or worse.

It's still early enough that the lot isn't full yet, though my eyes scan for Sebastian's Range Rover. Crap. There it is.

Even though school isn't packed yet and even with Frankie at my side, walking in is like taking some kind of risk. I can literally

31

feel the gossip as soon as I walk in the front door, like some kind of weird pervasive cloud of drama to push through. No one is exactly looking at me or saying anything, but they all know and I get enough side eyes to make me feel like I've got a cartoon blinking sign over my head in that hey-she-broke-up-with-her-longtime-boyfriend-who-had-another-girl-in-his-bed way. Nothing like small town schools, where everyone's life is everyone's business.

Frankie sticks right by my side. I've got a thick skin so I toss my shoulders back and cross the hallway as if nothing has changed in my life. Eyes forward, do not look for Sebastian. It's bad enough I have one class with him later. I don't need to see him now. Goal one: make it to my locker.

It's going to be a long day.

"Phew." I spin the dial on my locker. "That was awkward."

Frankie's eyes fill with tears. "I am so upset you're going through this."

I shrug. "Is what it is, right?"

"It's not fair." She blinks, her dark eyes wide with concern. She does her deep in thought, nervous habit of rearranging her bangs over her slightly too big forehead. It's a habit she's had since we were little kids and she'd get nervous around boys she had crushes on or when she thought her parents were mad at her.

I shrug again. "Just going to try and push through and not think about it. I need to talk to Ms. Hudson ASAP anyway. I missed the Get Up and Go trip and I need to find out if there's any way for me to be back in the running."

"Damn. I forgot about that." She frowns. "And how's Danny today?"

"Better."

"Good. Hudson will come through for you—"

"Jazz?" Sebastian's deep voice cuts through our conversation and I'm all bottom-falling-out-of-the-earth inside. But I turn around.

"May I help you?" I lace my voice with about ten tons of sarcasm as I cross my arms. But the arm crossing? It's barely holding me together.

Frankie takes a step back, her gaze darting between us. Again with the bangs being rearranged.

"How's Danny?" he asks, all genuine too. And don't get me wrong, Sebastian does care about my family. But I'm not falling back under his emotional spell.

"What do you want, Seb?"

"I want to know how your brother is." He has the nerve to say it incredulously, too, as if my refusing to tell him about my brother's hospital stay is me being a jerk. Even him mentioning my brother's name starts a low boil in me. He may have been part of my life, part of my family, for close to a year, but he's not now. So he doesn't get that right to know how any of us are doing.

"How's your new girlfriend?" I retort. My nerves are like jumping jacks on speed but I keep my face as blank as possible.

The color drains from his face and while my heart still feels like it's gone ten rounds in a boxing ring and lost every one, I have to admit, seeing him squirm feels pretty damn good.

Sebastian looks left and right. "Can we talk about this somewhere else?"

I realize he's right about me sort of making a scene. People are watching, even if they're pretending not to.

"Why?" I cock my head and pretend to be innocent.

He rubs a hand down his face, his expression changing from worried to plain old pissed. "Grow up, Jasmine. You know, you never gave me hardly more than a kiss. What did you expect?" He turns around and storms off.

My insides are in full earthquake mode. I turn back to my locker and dig through random piles of stuff on the bottom shelf to keep me busy and hidden. I squeeze my eyes shut and hope no one heard what he said.

"How dare he! Is he even for real?"

"Don't," I answer. I can't listen to Frankie, or anyone else's, sympathy. If I'm going to keep myself together, I need to create a new reality. One in which Sebastian Young never even existed.

"I need to go see Ms. Hudson. Catch you at lunch?"

Frankie puts a hand on my forearm. "Are you sure you're okay?"

"I'm fine!" When I smile as big as I can, Frankie's eyes narrow. I'm not fooling her.

She nods slowly. "Yep. See you then. Besties?"

"Forever," I reply.

MS. HUDSON SHARES an office with the band director. Being the teeny school that we are—our junior class has like 65 people in it—a lot of the extracurriculars have been cut, or at the very least, pared down to almost nothing. I'm actually kind of in shock that television and radio electives still exist considering they've toyed with cutting so many other programs, but, Ms. Hudson fights for us, and her ties to some of the New York radio stations give Easton High a bit of prestige, or something like that.

Let's hope those ties give me an in, too.

Have I mentioned how much I *need* that internship?

I knock softly.

When Ms. Hudson opens her door, I'm instantly filled with the everything-is-going-to-be-fine feeling she almost always gives me. Which doesn't even really make sense, considering my life is a big ole pile of everything-is-not-fine-at-all.

She's wearing one of her typical outfits, and I don't mean that in a mean way. It's just that Ms. Hudson is kind of stuck in the clothes of her heyday, the 80s, and that whole era has some strange looking stuff. Like today's outfit, a leatherette pencil skirt and an off the shoulder pink shirt. Her earrings have the circumference of a soda can but they complement her face well. Her blond hair is pulled back today, highlighting her heart shaped face. I mean, she's obviously older, but you can tell she was one of those kind of dorky, but cute girls when she was younger. She ushers me into her office, which, like I said, she shares with the band director. So it's half his stuff and some of hers. I look at the photos on the wall, like always. Ms. Hudson with some of the biggest radio names of the 80s and 90s. I sigh and fall into my seat.

"You look terrible!" she says.

Oh yeah, Ms. Hudson is really blunt too.

I don't even know where to start. Tears suddenly burn my eyes and I try to blink them away.

"I'm sorry," I say, swiping a finger under my eyes. "Monday was pure hell and I can't even believe I missed the Get Up and Go trip. Have I lost all hope of applying for the internship?"

Ms. Hudson purses her lips. "We'll see what we can do. I had a feeling something horrible had gone on. You aren't one to miss school for no reason and I know how excited you were for that trip."

"Beyond excited," I sniffle.

"So what happened?"

I launch into the whole sordid tale. Because I can be totally honest with Ms. Hudson, I even tell her about the girl I found with Sebastian. By the time I get through the hospital ride, my mom getting called into work and my sitting bedside with Danny all night, her face has fallen into an extreme look of pity, her mouth turned down in that deep frown she gets when she's particularly sad or upset, with her eyes crinkling and studying me like I'm a problem that needs solving. Pity is one thing I definitely do not want. I can handle myself.

"So anyway," I say, fighting my voice to regain some strength. "As you can see, missing the WYN60 trip and internship application thing was way out of my control. If there is any way possible for me to still go for it, I would pretty much do anything to at least try."

Ms. Hudson scrolls through her iPhone, pretty much the only proof in her life that the eighties are in fact over. "Many of the folks that were in the business when I left are now retired, but I do know the producer really well. She's the one who set up Monday's trip. I'll text her now and see if I can call her after school. Will you be available if she wants to conference you in?"

My body thrums with instant joy at even the hope of this phone call happening.

"Of course! Let me know."

She pulls me into a tight hug. "Everything will work out for you, Jasmine. Even if it doesn't feel like it now. This is a hard time for you, but you're one of the strongest girls I've ever had the pleasure to teach."

My eyes burn again.

The crackle of the intercom system makes me jump. Wow, I'm on freaking edge.

"Jasmine Torres, please come to the office. Jasmine Torres to the office."

A loud groan escapes me and I swallow the lump in my throat.

What the hell now?

5

I READ GUIDANCE counselor Mr. Fielding's scrawled message a few times. Naturally, it's from my mother. God. I crumple the note in my fist and toss it in the office garbage can on my way out. Apparently she got called into work early, for the afternoon shift, so she wants me to be home in time for Danny's bus. So she called to excuse me early. I mean, seriously? I've been out for two days and now leaving early? There goes my possible call with Ms. Hudson and the radio people.

I'm two parts blood boiling and one part close to tears. Is there anything she doesn't manage to ruin?

I'm still brooding as I make my way to my next class. I'll have to find a second between classes to tell Ms. Hudson to pick a different time for the call. This sucks.

I yawn through all my morning classes, but luckily, most of the teachers leave me alone. At lunchtime, I realize I forgot to pack lunch or bring money just as I'm reaching the cafeteria. I scrounge up two dollars from the bottom of my backpack and get in line for a bagel.

As I'm walking toward the courtyard with my bagel bag and milk, my eyes scan the room. Frankie is nowhere to be seen, which is no surprise. She has gym before lunch and with the amount of makeup and perfectly coordinated outfits Frankie wears, she takes a long time to get put back together. I push the door open and step into the warm day. I settle under the biggest tree—a magnolia. It's green now, the flowers all gone, but it's still my favorite. The courtyard is the best place to eat. The tables that line the large area are already filled, and more than a few people lounge under some of the other shade trees. But no Frankie yet.

As I'm unwrapping the bagel and opening the book we're reading in English—*The Invisible Man*, which, I have to admit, is pretty good—my mouth almost drops open when I hear a squeaky, syrupy-sweet voice.

"Give it back!"

It's her.

My head whips to the side, my gaze sweeping the courtyard. Great. And him. There they are, Sebastian and mystery girl, sitting at one of the side tables, her lying on the bench with her head in his lap, looking up at him. He smiles down at her and tweaks her nose.

Puke.

I turn my back to them, letting my hair fall like a curtain to hide my face, which feels like it's on fire. Breathe, Jasmine. Don't cry.

So basically, he had the nerve to come up to me at my locker this morning and act like he gave a crap about me or my family, and now here he is with her? Appetite gone, I shove the bagel back in the bag and lean against the tree trunk, studying my book as if it's got the answers to my life scrawled on its pages. I'm not about to leave this courtyard. I'm certainly not being driven out by them. I blink furiously against my gathering tears, thankful for my dark sunglasses.

Eleven months. That's how long we dated. I mean, he was my first boyfriend, first kiss. I think of his comment this morning. So what if we never got as far physically as Sebastian always wanted to go? Is that really a reason to find someone else? Whatever. Looks like I made the right decision about that after all. Shallow bastard. My heart is wrung out just thinking about how much I cared about him, that I thought I maybe even loved him. Never again will I trust someone so quickly.

When Frankie finally steps outside, swinging her bright paisley lunch bag, her eyebrows go so high, they're completely hidden under her bangs.

"Really?" She practically yells. Frankie does not know the meaning of an inside voice. She flops down on the grass next to me. "Is he even serious right now?"

Still yelling.

"Shhhh. Can we not alert every single person out here to the awkwardness of the situation?"

"As if it's not obvious?"

"Fantastic. Really." I groan.

"I'm just saying!"

"Shhhhh! Please stop. I know you're trying to help, but talking about him makes me want to throw up." I lie back on the grass, resting my open book on my chest. I flip my glasses back down over my eyes. "Who is she, anyway?" I whisper.

"She's a freshman, I think? I'm pretty sure she is the youngest of the Lanes."

"Ah, I *can* kind of see the resemblance." The Lane family has a zillion kids, which until now I had thought were all boys, all of which already graduated.

"I think her name is Alexa. I'm pretty sure she runs on the cross country team. Don't worry, I'll dig for more. Please tell me she isn't *the* one. Is she?" She flops down on the grass next to me and lowers her voice. "The one, one? The one you found him with?"

I nod.

Please don't let me throw up out here in front of everyone.

"Good God," Frankie says. I turn toward her as she continues to shake her head. "Sebastian is an ass."

"Obviously."

"Obviously." She unwraps her sandwich slowly and takes a bite. "She's got nothing on you. She's not even pretty. And listen to her. Obviously she's annoying as hell."

I groan. "Don't bother to try to make me feel better."

Frankie sighs. "I'm sorry. What else can I do? Let's do something fun. Want to hang out after school?"

"Can't. I have to be home for Danny."

"Where's Elena?"

Frankie is the only one who refers to my mom by her first name.

"Working."

She bites her lip. Frankie doesn't like to say bad stuff about my mom, but she knows me better than anyone so she knows what's up. Frankie has known me since before my dad left even, so she remembers Mom before she was like this. Sometimes I think she feels the brunt of Mom's demise almost as much as I do.

"I know, I know. I miss two days and now have to leave early. Not only that, but Hudson was going to try and conference me in to a call with WYN60 about the internship." I sigh.

"Oh my God, you can't miss—"

"I'll tell her to move it," I say. "It's for Danny."

She nods solemnly and looks out across the courtyard. More people spill onto the lawn, groups gathered in clumps on the grass and tables, laughing, joking, having fun in the admittedly perfect day. But of course I can't enjoy a second of it.

Even though Sebastian and freshman girl are behind me, their presence burns into my back like some kind of laser beam of misery. It's not even that I want to be the one giggling on his lap and looking up into his eyes, because I don't. Even with my hurt feelings and squashed perceptions of what my relationship actually was, I can say honestly that I do not want him. I just want

40

none of it to have happened. My heart is tattered and flapping in my very empty, endless cavern of a chest.

I squint into the sun and breathe as deeply as I can. Things will turn around soon. I know it.

6

AVOIDING SEBASTIAN GETS easier as the days and weeks pass. We still have our one class together, but I sit in the front row and pretend he doesn't exist. I have no idea if he's still seeing what's her name, but I try to ignore the mere existence of my ex-boyfriend. Okay, ignore isn't quite the right word considering the gashes on my heart feel like they are just starting to scab. But I'm doing a good impression of not caring and finding other stuff to think about.

It's not all that hard to distract myself. I'm caught up in waiting for Ms. Hudson to come through with the radio interview. Since Mom made me miss my chance at the after school phone interview, Ms. Hudson has not been able to find a good time that works for the producer to talk with me. I went ahead and applied for it and sent in my preliminary broadcast clips, but it's been two weeks since my should-have-been field trip and I'm no closer to getting my foot in the door at WYN60. It would be one thing if any of the other internships I applied for had even responded, but at this late stage in the game I'm pretty sure no news means bad news. Ms. Hudson and her connections are pretty much my only hope. Plus, come on, it's WYN60.

I'm in my second-to-last period when I get called to the office. By the time I get downstairs my palms are sweaty and my breathing comes in short spurts. It's been a few weeks and, I realize now, I've begun to let my guard down.

Please let Danny be okay.

The secretary at the front desk smiles at me. "Hello, Jasmine. Your mom left a phone message for you. No emergency, dear."

Even with her kind words, I can't turn off my racing fear, and I take the paper with shaking fingers.

I exhale as I read Mom's note. She's excusing me to leave early once again, to get home for Danny. She got called into work and I need to take him to his follow up at the neurologist.

Annoying how she thinks I can leave school whenever her schedule demands it. But at least Danny is okay.

And besides, silver lining, at least she's leaving me her car for the afternoon. I tuck the note into my pocket just as my cell phone buzzes. I duck into the bathroom to look at it. The cell phone rules aren't as strict in the hall as they are in class, but I don't want to take a chance so near the main office.

It's a text from Ms. Hudson.

Good news! Call with WYN60 tomorrow morning. Can you come to school a little early?

My stomach leaps. This is amazing. Can I come early? Of course! I have to. Mom will have to handle things with Danny in the morning.

YES! I type back, unable to keep the smile from my face.

I LOVE DRIVING Mom's car. It's an old beat up thing, a hatchback Civic from like decades ago. But it has a good radio and, hey, it's a car. After mostly walking, especially now that I've lost Sebastian as my ride most places, I'd drive a rusted out jalopy if it meant getting around.

Danny sits back in his booster seat, listening to his iPod. He bops his head and looks out the window, calmed as usual by his music. He's quiet most of the ride and I navigate the roads that lead to his doctor's office.

"It's the Beatles, Jazzy!" Danny yells.

I smile absently as I stop at a red light. "Don't yell, I can hear you even though your music is loud!"

"What?" He bobs his head and hums loudly. I wave away his question and watch him in the mirror. His blinks become slower, longer. He seems tired, like he almost always does after school. As long as that's all it is. I turn onto the highway, distracted by my worry.

He nods off and is asleep by the time we reach the doctor's office. He grudgingly climbs out of the car, dragging the toes of his sneakers along the sidewalk and down the long hallway inside.

"I don't get why we have to come here again? Didn't I just go to the hospital?" He crosses his arms and stops short in the hallway. "I'm sick of coming here."

I sigh and run my hands through my hair. Cranky Danny is no good for any of us. And he's right. He shouldn't have to be here. But I don't think a Life Is Unfair lecture is going to do any of us any good.

"Sorry kiddo," I say, resting my hand on his shoulder. "I know it's only been a few weeks since your hospital visit, but Dr. Bee likes to check up on her favorite patients. Believe me, I wish you didn't have to be here either."

It's true, of course. Him having to be here at all just about breaks my heart. Best neurologists around—I'll give Mom credit for finding good doctors—but damn I wish he didn't have to be here.

He bites his lip, eying up the receptionist with contempt. I steer him toward the fish tank in one of the waiting rooms.

"Tell you what," I say. "You hang out here while I sign you in. If we get out of here in decent time, we can check out that new playground?"

"The pirate one?" His eyes light up.

"Yep. The pirate one. With the little adventure course?"

He nods sharply. "Fine."

"But you have to cooperate. No complaining, okay?"

He scowls.

"And no scowling, either."

A small smile quivers on his lips.

"What is that I see?" I sing song, as his smile widens. He tries to keep a straight face, but can't. I squeeze his shoulder again and make my way to the reception window, happy to have diverted a true tantrum. Danny is a mostly agreeable kid, but with tired Danny it could go either way. He watches the fish in the tank while I stand in line.

"Jazzy!" he calls as I hand over Mom's insurance card.

"One second, Dan," I mutter as I fill out the sign in sheet.

"The fish are bigger, Jazzy. Come see. There are new ones too!" My brother's smile is genuine now, and I say a silent thanks to the heavens that his mood has shifted. When the receptionist hands back my card, I thank her and head over to the waiting room where Danny has practically pressed his entire skinny body against the huge glass fish tank.

"Oh wow." I squat down to look at the fish from his viewpoint.

"Sunny?"

Wait.

I turn around and sure enough, Wesley, the boy from Danny's hospital room, sits in a chair against the far wall.

For real?

"Wes, right?"

His freckled cheeks lift when his mouth quirks up on one side. He's got one of those smiles you can tell is exactly how he looked when he was a little kid. Mischievous. Even the flop of hair on his forehead says he's probably up to no good.

"You remembered me," he says.

"Oh. Well, you remembered me first."

"Not every pretty girl is mean to random strangers who happen to be hospital patients. For the record. It makes you pretty memorable."

"Come on! I was not mean. If I recall, it was the other way around. You were making fun of me."

"I can hardly be counted on to be chivalrous from a hospital bed."

Which reminds me. Here we are. He's a patient here too. I wonder what his story is, but I don't want to ask. Suddenly, the silence is awkward as I look around.

"Is your mom here too?"

"My mom?" his eyes widen. "Wow. I really am striking out on keeping your attention if you're asking about my mom."

My face burns. "No. It's just that I met her, at the hospital. She was nice."

"Yeah, she's fine. But tell me about you."

That easy, he asks. Why can't I be that smooth?

I glance over at Danny, still standing pressed against the glass, tracing the paths of the fish. I motion to him.

"Danny has a follow up from the St. Bonaventure adventure."

"Same here," Wes says.

"Are you a patient of Dr. Bee too?"

"Yep. Since I was five or so."

I nod.

"Seizure disorder, epilepsy." Wes adds.

I look down at my shoes. I don't know why, but his honesty makes me feel exposed.

"Same for us." I nod to Danny again, sitting at one of the game tables, now, pushing beads along the wire frames. "He had a bad one that week. So, there we were."

Wes frowns. He tosses his head back to flip his hair out of his eyes. When he looks at me, mischief dances in them again. "But, you did meet me, right? So it wasn't a total loss."

I consider his words. It's weird in a way, him downplaying Danny's hospitalization. But if I'm being honest, it's refreshing, too.

"Not quite a silver lining," I say, tapping a finger against my lips. "Silver lining would have been meeting, I don't know, Dylan O'Brien or something?"

"Dylan O'Brien, really?"

"Yeah. Completely. Or even, maybe winning like a two dollar scratch off lottery ticket."

Wes narrows his eyes. "A two dollar lottery ticket?" he deadpans. "Would have been better than meeting me?"

My grin starts to widen. "It's an apples and oranges comparison, really. Two bucks is two bucks."

He opens his mouth to respond, his eyes glinting with that childish gleam again.

"Mr. McEnroe?" The nurse in the doorway looks out at us. Wes stands.

"Yeah. That's me."

"This way," she says disappearing through the door. He moves to follow and I'm filled with a sudden sense of, I don't know, being let down? I'm not sure exactly why though. He's fun to talk to. But also, meeting him by chance—twice? And… there he goes.

Oh well.

"Good luck," I say.

"Thanks." He disappears behind the nurse and my heart falls a little bit. Which is dumb. I barely know him. But still, he made me laugh. And for those few minutes? He was a good distraction.

I move Danny's pile of books from the seat beside me. "Hey Dan, want me to read you one of these?"

My brother looks up at me as if noticing me for the first time. "When I'm done!" he answers, tongue caught between his teeth as he concentrates on a logic puzzle with beads and wires.

Okay then. I pull out my phone, curious to see if Mom even bothered to check in with me about Danny's visit. Missed calls: 0. Texts: 0. Way to go, Mom.

The nurse's door opens again. Hopefully, it's our turn.

Wes dashes out, and stops in front of me. "Sunny," he says. "Coffee?"

"Excuse me?"

He huffs impatiently, but his eyes still have that been-smiling-my-whole-life look in them.

"Mr. McEnroe?" The nurse's voice, much more impatient now, drifts from the hallway beyond.

"Come on, I'm going to get in trouble. You aren't going to insult me again, are you? I'm worth less than two bucks, I know. And you kick a guy when he's down, scream at him while he's hospitalized…"

"Would you stop that? I did not. But I'm confused. What did I do now?"

"Coffee," he says. "Me, you. Getting coffee. Maybe even some dessert to go with it. You do eat dessert… Please tell me you eat dessert?"

"Yeah, of course. Who doesn't eat dessert?"

"You'd be surprised. So? Coffee? *And* I'll make sure you don't burn yourself this time."

"Um… sure. Yeah, I guess?"

"Ouch. *Sure yeah I guess?*" He shakes his head all mock sad. Then as if to himself, "I have definitely lost my touch somewhere along the way."

"No! I didn't mean it like that. Sorry. It's been kind of a crazy day. Week. Life. I don't know. Holy foot in mouth Jasmine." And *then* I have the audacity to further insult my character by wincing and barking out my horrible nervous laugh, the one reserved for really awkward moments like when I tried to pull out a pen at lunch and a tampon went flying across the cafeteria in front of everyone, and I mean everyone, like the whole junior and senior class. I can almost still hear the snickers and shocked silence.

Wes stares at me, wide eyed.

"What?" I ask.

"So... are you going to give me your number? Because I don't know about other people, but just so you know, the seizures I have personally did not, unfortunately, give me any psychic abilities."

Oh my God.

"What? Oh! Sure." I whip out my cell. "What's your number? I'll text you."

"Nice. A girl who knows what she wants. I like it." His grin widens again and I roll my eyes.

"Now you're just being stupid," I smirk.

The nurse's voice calls again from beyond the door and he nods toward it, giving me wide, hurry up eyes. But he gives me the number and I quickly text him so he'll have mine.

Hi. I write. *It's Jasmine.*

He glances down at his phone with a smile before disappearing from the waiting room doorway.

7

I GET TO school super early the next day for my conference call with Ms. Hudson and her contact at the radio station. Even though it's only a phone call, my palms are sweating like crazy. When I wipe them on my capris, the comforting jingle of my favorite bangles calms me as Ms. Hudson dials the phone.

When her friend answers, they banter for a bit and small talk about the good old days, before Ms. Hudson gives me a smile and motions for me to come closer to the speakerphone. I sit across the desk from her and she places the phone between us, on a stack of music books.

"So, Roberta. I'd like to virtually introduce you to one of my star students. She is an absolute delight on the air. Her name is Jasmine Torres. I suspect you received her application and clips?"

"Hi there, Jasmine! I'm sure we did." A friendly voice comes through the speaker.

"Hi! It's so nice to meet you. Well, not officially meet you, but, well, you know."

I bite the inside of my cheek. Shut up, Jasmine.

"Jasmine was supposed to be at the trip a few weeks ago, but she had a family emergency and unfortunately had to miss it."

"I'm sorry to hear that," the voice says. "I hope everything is okay."

"Thanks," I say. "I appreciate that. I was really upset to miss the trip. I was really looking forward to it. Radio is, like, all I care about. It's my dream!"

Can I sound any more stupid?

"So we are calling to see if there is any way possible we can schedule a time to talk," Ms. Hudson says, using a careful and professional voice. "As we already mentioned, Jasmine has sent in an application for the summer internship and I think you'd really like her. I know you probably don't have time to talk in depth with her now, but if we could set up a time that is good for you, perhaps?"

"How about this," the woman says, papers rustling in the background. "I have an opening Monday after next. By that time, we will certainly have narrowed down all the applications and the physical interviews will have started. Why doesn't Jasmine come in for an in-person meeting? I'd love to meet you, Ms. Torres, and possibly show you around a bit."

Monday after next. My mind races, darting from home to Danny to Mom to school. How can I do this? No matter how, I have to make it work. Fake it till you make it will work just fine this minute anyway. I'll figure out the details later.

"Sure!" I say. "That sounds great. Yes, I can definitely make that work."

By the time we hang up, we've managed to set up all the details of the meeting. Ms. Hudson is a freaking life saver and even offered to travel into the city with me to go to WYN60. To say I owe her huge is the understatement of the year. I practically skip out of her office. Perhaps all hope is not lost after all. Now, I just have to hope I have what it takes to beat out whatever other applicants they narrow it down to.

Even though there's still forty minutes until first bell, Frankie is waiting by my locker when I get there. I smile and pull her into an exaggerated hug that is way more her style than mine. I

51

even dance a little while we're hugging, which makes her break into laughter.

"So I guess it went well?" She grins.

"Better than well! The lady, Roberta, from WYN60 is willing to meet with me for a private interview for the internship. Hudson's going to go into the city with me. Monday the 15th."

"Sweet. I knew Hudson would make it happen!"

"It's just a meeting. There are no guarantees. Plus, she said they'll be interviewing other applicants by then too."

"Come on! Enjoy the moment. This could be huge."

My smile widens and bubbles of excitement inch through my belly.

Frankie's face turns serious. "How's Danny?"

"Better. They upped his meds. Fingers crossed." My phone buzzes in my pocket and I pull it out. Wes's name lights up the screen and I can't help it, I smile.

"Don't even tell me," Frankie says, her nose scrunched in disgust.

I look up. "What?"

"You didn't take him back, did you?"

"Take who back?"

"Um, Sebastian, you know, boyfriend of almost a year who you recently broke up with? Don't lie to me. I'm your best friend, remember. I'll see through your crap. I know that little smile."

I slam my locker. Absolutely nothing can get me in a bad mood today.

"Who says it's Sebastian?" I say, as coyly as I can manage. "There are millions of boys in the world you know." And with that, I take off down the hall, leaving Frankie with her mouth open behind me. I scroll to Wes's text and grin at the picture of a Starbucks coffee cup.

coffee date soon?

Seeing the word date makes my stomach clench, worse than the first time I was live on the air, even. I am so not ready for anything remotely like that. Not a date. But I still can't help smiling as I text him back.

perhaps.

I type as Frankie skids to a stop beside me. She puts a hand on my arm.

"Please," she says, all out of breath like the track star she most definitely is not. "Please tell me you aren't messing with me and that is an actual boy that is *not* Sebastian that you are texting?"

"Yep." I nod.

I relish the look of pure astonishment Frankie gives me. It's rare I can shock my best friend.

"What? Who? How?" She sputters.

"I'm completely late," I say. "I promise to fill you in later."

She huffs. "Come on! Give me *something*."

"I met him at the hospital. He goes to the same doctor as Danny."

Frankie's eyes go all bug-eyed wide. "What! And you didn't tell me?"

"I didn't really think anything of it, and then…"

"And then he's texting you and you're all goo goo smiling."

"I'm not goo goo smiling! At all. Come on, I broke up with Sebastian, what, a few weeks ago? I mean, it's not like I want him back, or whatever, but I'm not about to jump into something else right now."

"Mm hmm. But tell me about *him*." She nods to my phone.

"Later, I promise."

"A name at least?"

"Wes. Come on, I told Ms. Hudson I'd up the editing quality on my recordings for my portfolio for the interview. She's blocked off the studio for me during study period and I get to broadcast the morning show today so I gotta get to work."

Frankie squeezes my arm before I turn away. "First period, then. I want all the details. Go do your thing. I'll be listening!"

Rushing down the hall, I turn into the arts wing and head for the studio. When I close the studio door behind me, my pulse slows as I step into the familiar surroundings. Ahhh. It's like coming home. Better than actually, when you consider my current home situation.

The studio is my ultimate space. It's a small room, taken up mostly by a rectangular table in the middle, three chairs, a few mics and computer monitors. But it's got cool, retro-style desk lamps in rainbow colors, for when you don't want to use the overhead. Even though the microphones and the soundboard are old, they're real radio station stuff. So it feels very official. No matter what's going on when I slide into the chair in front of the main mic, I can never keep the smile off my face or the flutter of excitement from my veins. And even though we use only digital music now, the walls are still lined with crates of CDs and even albums that were donated over the years, making the room cozy and colorful. The walls that aren't stacked with music have various radio station posters. More pictures of Ms. Hudson and all sorts of recording artists are framed here too.

Easton High may be small, but we do manage to maintain our own dedicated radio station. It broadcasts before and after school, as well as lunch periods. You can only catch it in the cafeteria and study rooms over speakers, but we're also on Easton 1620 AM a few hours a day, which comes in for about a twenty-mile radius. Pretty cool.

Because there aren't a ton of radio students, it's not always manned during the radio show hours, so we do play a lot of pre-recorded segments.

I text Wes back a smiley face while I get the equipment set up. Turning on the computer, I adjust the microphone and jam the broken band of my headphones together well enough to stay put before sliding them over my ears. Twenty minutes until classes start means students will be arriving or on their way. The breakfast kids are probably already down in the cafeteria.

"Good morning Easton High!" Warmth envelopes me as I talk into the mic. "It's Thursday morning and we are one day closer to the weekend. I'm gonna kick it back with some old school summer jams. Coming your way to bring us back to the sandy days down the shore, here are the Beach Boys."

I start the song, click the microphone off, and sit back in my seat with a smile. Any stress I was feeling before walking into this room melts away like I'm on the beach myself. No, actually, this room? Better than the beach any day.

I check the screen to make sure the show is recording and get ready for my talk segment. I laugh nervously at what I have planned, but I'm going to go for it.

My phone dings again.

so...tonight?
perhaps, i said. can't u read?;)

I laugh as the phone dings again. Wes.

i see

And then:

no dessert for u. :p

When the last song of my set ends, I pull the microphone toward me. "Hope ya'll are awake out there, Easton. Today we are talking about relationships. Do you have one? Have you ended one? Are you looking for one or running as far away from commitment as fast as you can? Email me at Eastonmornings at Easton dot edu and tell me your story. Let's start with the worst break up stories. If you've got one, bring it my way. And in the meantime, here's a song on that theme, which I am officially declaring the theme of the morning."

I hit play on Taylor Swift's "We Are Never Ever Getting Back Together" and sit back in my chair with a grin. My stomach squeezes like it's being wrung out by two iron fists. I know it's a low blow to Sebastian, but I couldn't resist. Even if I'm slowly starting to heal, he deserves it. In here, in my Easton Mornings DJ chair, I'm untouchable.

My phone buzzes. Must be Wes again.

It's Sebastian.

Eek.

Really, J?

I don't answer. Screw him. He's the one who got caught with another girl. He deserves to feel like crap *and* a little bit of covert humiliation.

Another buzz. Wes.

so? tonight. yes or no? check one, lol.

I smile.

whҽrҽ do you go to school? I type.
what? u want to know what I'm wearing?
haha. um... no.

babylon. he writes. **u?**

easton. ur close, then. what are you doing right now?

um, right this minute? cramming for a history exam i forgot about. ha.

are you home or in ur car?

my car. just pulled up to school.

turn on your radio.

wait, what?

it's an a.m. station. 1620.

why?

just do it. boy, u suck at following directions.

very funny.

just listen to it.

um? ok. finding it now...

BRB

I switch back to the microphone as the song comes to a close. "Good morning guys and gals. If you're just tuning in, we were talking this morning about tough break ups. The email is blowing up and I want to thank you, Easton High School, for sharing your stories with me." I scan my computer quickly. "Here's one from someone identifying themselves as Heartbroken Fifteen. This listener was broken up with by text message and then blocked from her boyfriend's phone before she could even respond. Man, that is rough. I've heard some bad ones, especially lately, you wouldn't believe it if I told you, but wow, that is low. Hope you're moving on, Heartbroken Fifteen. You definitely deserve better. Keep the stories coming in, listeners. This is Jasmine Torres, bringing you all your favorite before-school jams. And now, this next song goes out to a friend of mine. Hey, Wes, listen up. This one is for you since I know you're a huge Justin Bieber fan."

I hit the button to play Bieber's latest. As soon as my mic is off, I burst out laughing.

My phone, of course, buzzes.

OMG Is that seriously you on the radio
surprised?
very. there's more to Sunny than meets the eye.
u have no idea.

Don't ask where these comments came from. Like I said, being in the studio makes me all crazy confident like not a thing can go wrong in my world.

but bieber! really?
haha
oh u wait. revenge will be sweet. so... about that coffee date tonight????????
fine. I pause. but stop calling it a date. friends only.

I know, it sounds harsh. But I do not need another boy situation at this point.

friends it is.
:)

I smirk at the screen and lean into the microphone to finish my show.

"Hello again, Easton High! I'll be wrapping up after another song or two, so here is me, wishing all of you a very happy Thursday. Today, I think, is going to be a very good day, indeed."

I can only hope Wes is still listening. Sebastian too, for that matter.

I'M GRATEFUL I only have one class with Sebastian. But still, I can barely drag myself to last period English. The day has been buoyed by my good mood, impending internship interview with Get Up and Go, and coffee with my new friend tonight. That's if I'm right and Mom is not working as per usual Thursday nights.

Please, please, universe, give me this.

But when I walk into English, my eyes scan the room. All the good feelings drain as quickly as if a stopper has been pulled out of me, when I see Sebastian in his corner seat. He's looking down at his lap with a smirk. Probably texting someone.

Good mood, gone.

Mr. James is at his desk. He's a mess, as usual, briefcase spilling papers all over, glasses practically dangling from the end of his nose. I smile, trying to ignore the pit of worry gnawing my stomach at the thought of having to spend forty five minutes in the same room as Sebastian.

Whatever.

I stop at Mr. James' desk. I missed class yesterday and even though he's one of my nicest teachers, being that English isn't my best subject, I have to work harder here than I do in my other classes. Given my love of reading, you'd think I'd have some innate ability to do well in the subject, but alas, no. I just hope I didn't miss a massive project or assignment or anything that will tank my weekend. Mr. James is very fond of projects.

"Aha!" He says with his usual dramatic flourish. "She finally arrives. How was your day off, Ms. Torres?"

"So sorry." I duck my head. "Family stuff. I had to leave early yesterday."

His face softens. "Everything okay?"

I nod. Mr. James is super nice, but except for Ms. Hudson, I try to keep my family drama out of school.

"We were working on a new group presentation project. You can work with Trina's group," he says, rooting around in his briefcase.

Group presentations? Please universe, *do not* put me in a group with Sebastian.

"Here it is!" He pulls out a crumpled piece of paper and smiles triumphantly, waving it like a flag. I laugh, despite myself. Mr. James is crazy, in a funny way though, like a family friend whose antics entertain at parties but who you're thankful isn't related to you.

"I am," he says with a dramatic, hand sweeping bow. "*The Invisible Man.* Not really, but that's the book we're reading, as you hopefully know and have been reading. Anyhow. Here's a list of questions to choose from. Your group has probably already started some, but you can decide among yourselves which others you may want to answer. You'll report to the class by Monday of next week."

I take the paper and walk to the corner of the room where Trina sits. My stomach drops out like one of those free fall rides at Great Adventure. The ones I hate.

You have to be kidding me.

My feet stutter like I'm just learning to walk. I have to force them to do that one in front of the other thing they've been doing for much of my seventeen years.

Of course Sebastian is in Trina's group. Of course I'd be forced to work with him. Sigh.

Universe, 1. Jasmine, 0.

"Oh my God," Trina is saying to Sebastian as I drag a desk over to them. "I'm still on chapter one, I am so useless on this project."

"You know I already read it. I did all the work yesterday too." Sebastian huffs, his lips turning down in a frown. Those lips I've kissed so many times. Deep breath. I can do this.

"Hey guys," I say. "I'm apparently joining your group. And no worries, Trina. I read it too."

"Hey, Jasmine! I heard your radio show this morning. So awesome. You're so incredibly good at it. I would completely choke up and have no idea what to say."

"Thanks," I say with a genuine smile as I slide into the desk. I scoot slightly closer to Trina. I may have to work with him, but if I don't look at him or smell his cologne, I can pretend he's just any guy in our group.

"Yeah." Sebastian deadpans. "I loved the Taylor Swift song."

Gulp. Okay, maybe not just any guy.

"Thanks so much, Sebastian, that is so nice of you to say." I keep my voice sweet as sugar and, I'm going to admit it right now, even if my pulse is off the charts fast and even if being near my ex is sort of making me want to both fold up and cry and stand up and scream, I kind of love the way his face turns tomato red in anger.

I'm a mess.

Trina looks back and forth between us. Obviously, she isn't a link in the Easton High gossip chain.

"So, what question are we working on first?" I ask, feigning sudden interest in *The Invisible Man*. I did finish it, so I should be able to contribute, but really, I just want Sebastian to get that dark look off his face.

He taps the edge of his notebook with his pen. I watch his fingers, considering how many times I've held them, how many times they've massaged my neck or rubbed circles on the back of my hand. Damn it. The ache of what he did swells again, like it did the day I found him with that girl, and I'm momentarily blinded by it. But Taylor Swift had it right. I honestly do not want him back, even if questions about how it all went down bob endlessly in the sea of my emotions.

Trina sighs. "You guys are always so smart and ahead of the game. I've totally had my head up my ass the last two weeks with the Hello Summer carnival thing."

Sebastian rolls his eyes, just barely. He hates all school events so this is no shock. But I realize suddenly that thanks to him, I've missed out on plenty, too.

"When is it?" I ask.

She lets out a sound that's a cross between a squeal and a yell, her magenta lips wide in shock. "Oh my God, you are coming, right? You have to come. It's the last Friday in June. Last day of junior year, but together one last time. You guys can't miss it. You're totally a who's who of our class. You're like the longest running couple of our year, probably."

I clear my throat and look down at my paper. If I could broadcast a radio show from my head to hers it would say: *Hello listeners this is your newly single and liberated DJ, Jasmine Torres! Ix Nay on the Oyfriend Bay conversation.*

But of course, being Trina, bless her heart she is as nice as she is dumb, she completely missed any type of signal Sebastian and I are giving off. I can't believe she *still* hasn't heard the rumors. Girl lives in her own world, that's for sure.

"Sounds fun!" I say, which is a total lie. I hate carnivals. I can think of about a million reasons not to spend the afternoon in the school parking lot playing dumb games and eating greasy food. Of all the fun school events I missed when I was Sebastian's girlfriend, it would have been awesome if the first one I'll probably go to was something I actually wanted to do.

"Anyway," I say. "Let's get started on these questions."

8

WES AND I text no less than ten times before we figure out exactly where our coffee non-date is happening.

Since it's not a date, I'm not nervous. I mean, I'm meeting him for coffee. In a bookstore. Well, the bookstore's coffee area. Whatever. Nothing to be nervous about.

I wear a yellow polka dot sundress and my beaded leather sandals. Yep. My favorite outfit.

Which still doesn't make it a date.

Thankfully I was right about Mom having the night off. I give Danny his evening medicine and go over his homework. The kid is crazy smart, despite all his hurdles. I kiss the top of his head.

"You smell nice Jazzy."

"Thanks, Dan. How're you feeling?"

He rolls his eyes. "Same as I did when you asked five minutes ago. Fine. Why you always asking?" He sticks out his tongue.

I slap a big smile on my face, but inside, I crumble more than a little bit. I have to keep my worries to myself. Danny has already had enough to deal with in his short life. He doesn't need me making him even more paranoid about having another seizure.

Mom comes in, fresh out of the shower, her wet hair hanging halfway down her back. "You look nice," she says. "Going out?"

"Yeah. Out for coffee. With friends. Remember, you said I could borrow your car?"

"Oh yeah, that's right. Have fun." Her eyes dart around the kitchen as if she's nervous or looking for something.

"Danny's homework is done, but I didn't make dinner."

"That's fine, I'll heat something up. Want to watch a movie, kiddo?" She ruffles Danny's hair.

"My choice?"

"Sure, go ahead. We'll eat in there."

Danny sprints across the room, grabbing the remote from the counter on the way. He flops onto the couch and starts flipping through the channels while Mom pokes through the leftovers in the fridge. She pulls out a bottle of soda and a Styrofoam container. I watch as she mixes a drink with way more vodka than soda. With her back to me, she takes a long gulp.

My stomach turns.

"Hey Dan," she calls. "I'm going to reheat the hamburgers, how's that sound?"

"Good," he calls, the TV volume almost louder than his voice. "But none of that gross cheese."

"Um, Mom?" I swallow, eying her already half empty glass. I want to remind her to keep a close eye on Danny, a more or less sober eye.

She turns to me with a smile, eyes not glazed over yet.

"Forget it," I say. I don't want to fight with her before I leave. All that will do is upset Danny.

My cell phone rings in my room and I dash down the hall to get it.

I hope Mom doesn't drink too much while I'm out tonight. Maybe going out is a bad idea.

I reach the phone on the third ring. "Hey, Ms. Hudson!"

"Sorry to bother you at home. I listened to the recording of your morning show. Pretty good stuff there. Since we have the WYN60 meeting in less than two weeks, it would help if you could add some more to your portfolio. Want to do the morning show tomorrow too, and all of next week?"

I stop pacing and stare at myself in the mirror. Morning show all week? Hell yes. I can totally be the star for a week. Excitement bubbles in my stomach.

"As long as things are cool with my brother, I should be able to be there early enough to do it each day."

That's a big if, of course. Mom better cooperate and get her crap together. I adjust the straps on my sandals and give my dark hair one last once-over, scrunching my curls. I blend my eyeliner with my fingertip, trying for a less dramatic look.

"Perfect!" She says. "I'll let the others know we're changing the schedule. I'm sure they'll understand. You've been sounding good, Jasmine, but there are some kind of shaky segments I'd like to leave out of your portfolio. So try to really nail these next few, okay? You want to give yourself the best shot you can."

Shaky segments? Great.

"I'll be there tomorrow morning, then," I say, hoping I can pull it off.

We hang up and I head out the door with mom's keys. Sometimes Mom does come through, I admit to myself as I slide into her car. I back out of my driveway with a silent prayer that everything will work out tonight and Mom will keep a good eye on Danny.

HERE'S THE THING about non-dates at bookstores. Books. I get there earlier than Wes, so I stroll around looking at all the new releases. I thumb through a few that look decent and commit them to memory for my next library trip.

On my way to the magazines, I look outside. I wonder what kind of car he drives. Or if he drives. Lots of epilepsy patients can't drive, depending on how well their seizures are controlled with medication. I have spent three years worrying about the same thing for Danny when he grows up. But I don't know much about Wes's situation.

I think about the way he casually threw out his diagnosis with me at Dr. Bee's office yesterday. He's an open book, no freaking pun intended as I stand amongst thousands of them. I like that about him.

I squat down in the magazine aisle, flipping idly through *Teen Queen* magazine. I'm deep in a quiz about what my future job should be, trying to add up the score to each question while making sure not to wrinkle the pages. These stupid quizzes suck me in every time. I add the numbers in my head, falling squarely in the "creative job" category. I can live with that.

"Sunny!"

Wes's voice is way closer than I expect. With my balance being pretty crappy as it is, and squatting down the way I am, I have to grab the edge of the magazine rack to keep from falling.

"Hey." I pull myself up, trying to pretend like I wasn't about to fall over.

Wes pushes his hair back and gives me one of his side smiles. He's wearing a plain black tee shirt that's fitted enough to show off his physique. He's not really muscular, but he's got a good build. And the black looks really good with his coloring, making his natural blond highlights stand out.

"You look nice," he says, scratching the back of his head. He nods to my dress. "Sunny again."

I look down at myself and laugh. Yellow again. "So it is. And thanks." *You look nice too*, I'm tempted to add.

"Sorry I'm late," he says. "My friend was over and I couldn't get rid of him. I finally left him there, playing video games alone in my house."

"Alone in your house?"

"Sort of. My parents are home. Mom'll cook him dinner and let him hang out."

I laugh. "That's kind of odd."

"Yeah. Jacob is really a weirdo. He's like the quintessential frat boy, even though he's only in high school. His parents are pushing him for college and all that, but all he does is play video games. I don't think he's destined for more than beer pong champion."

"Ouch. Hope you don't talk about all your friends that way."

"What can I say, I'm honest. And don't worry, he says it about himself. Laziest guy around. Come on." He nods toward the café.

We wait in line behind a mother with four very noisy kids. One of them turns around and sticks his tongue out at us, more than once. I barely stifle my laugh. Beside me, Wes makes a funny face back at the kid, sticking his tongue out and crossing his eyes.

"Oh my God, Wes," I whisper, snorting a laugh.

I trace the edge of the dessert case while the line edges up toward the counter. We peer into the window like kids in a candy shop. "Everything looks so good," I say. "I'm definitely going for the double chocolate brownie."

When it's our turn he motions for me to order first. "Order it to go," he says. "We'll sit outside. If a famous radio DJ doesn't mind being seen with a lowly guy like me…"

I raise an eyebrow. "Hardly famous." I laugh as I pull out my wallet when the barista returns with my brownie and coffee. Wes nods to the register.

"Come on," he says. "I got this."

I hand the barista a five dollar bill. "I can pay for myself," I tell Wes.

"I don't see why you have to," he says as he orders chocolate chip cookies and the biggest coffee they've got.

67

We settle at one of the outside tables. It's ridiculously nice out. Not summer hot, but enough to stay light a little later and have that warmth about the evening that feels like being lazy and lying around in the grass.

I think about those summer nights a few years ago, when high school first started. Before Danny got sick. Sometimes I'd hang out at Frankie's and sit outside by the fire pit with her family until way after dark, roasting marshmallows and telling silly ghost stories. Those nights felt endless and even after her family went to bed, we'd stay up chatting in her room practically all night before finally falling asleep. We'd wake up so late the next morning and I'd eventually get home. There was no worry then about Danny needing me there to make sure he was okay, or make sure he got his medicine.

If I close my eyes and think back far enough, I can even remember summers way before that, when I was a little kid, before Danny was even born. I can almost even remember the way Mom's laugh sounded like pure music and how beautiful she was then, glowing as she and Dad danced to one of his old meringue albums. I can still see the turn of his hips and the fast movements of his feet. Mom could never follow the steps right and she'd fall against him, breathless and laughing.

I can almost still hear the meringue music.

He loved those albums so much. More than us, I guess, since he took all but a few of them and left us behind.

Despite the warm evening air, I shiver. I glance at my phone, hoping everything is okay with Mom and Danny. Maybe I should check in with her.

Wes, luckily, doesn't seem to notice. He takes a massive bite of his cookie.

"Hungry?" I ask, nibbling on my brownie. "Wow, this is good."

"Yeah. The double chocolates are my second favorite here."

"So you come here a lot?"

He grins. "Ah the old come-here-often pick up line. Nice one."

I ignore that. "So you go to Babylon? What's it like? Private schools have always intrigued me. Do you guys wear uniforms and play pranks on people all day? Do you play preppy sports like lacrosse and drink scotch and smoke cigars after your games?"

He laughs as he licks crumbs off his fingers. "Whoa, where are you getting your private school information? Cheesy movies? There's nothing special about private schools. I've always wished I could go to public, actually. First of all, no girls. Whose idea was it to put a bunch of high school guys in a building with no girls?" He grimaces in horror and I laugh.

"I'm sure you manage." I take a sip of my coffee.

He shrugs, a slight blush spreading across his cheeks. "There may have been a girlfriend or two."

"I figured as much. And the uniforms?"

"They're awful. But I don't drink scotch or smoke. And I don't play sports."

"Ah, kindred spirits. I'm not a sports girl either. So, what do you do for fun? Despite harass girls you meet in hospitals?"

He rolls his eyes. "Drink coffee, hang with my friends, play video games... I don't know. Normal stuff."

"And comics."

"Have you been stalking me? How did you know about my comics?"

Now it's my turn to blush. I guess I had been a little *too* observant. "I saw them in the hospital."

"So you *were* checking me out. I knew it." He grins. "Anyway, I'm boring. What about you? What's up with your radio show? That's so cool."

A spark lights in me at the mention of the Easton Mornings show. "Been helping out with the school station since freshman year. Now they let me broadcast alone sometimes, have my own mini show, almost. Like you heard yesterday. I'm going to the Get Up and Go show for a possible internship so my teacher is letting me broadcast alone for the next week or so to hopefully record some good segments to bring with us."

"So cool. We don't have anything like that at my school."

"Yeah, it's not a super common thing, but we have a really great radio teacher who keeps the program going. Some schools around here have it though. If you ever tune into 1530, you'll hear DJ Big Dee from Chester High."

Wes laughs. "Who's that? From the look on your face, not a close friend, I'm guessing?"

"Definitely not," I say. "She's kind of what you'd call my rival I guess. We've competed in DJ stuff before and I'm sort of cringing inside at the thought of her going for the same internship as me."

"Well I haven't heard DJ Big B, but—"

"D," I correct him, laughing.

"DJ Big D," he says. "Got it. D as in dork?"

"No, Dee as in Dee Ann. Dee Ann Walkins, to be exact. Senior at Chester High and, I have to admit, a pretty good DJ."

"Forget about Big Dee. I've heard you and you're pretty awesome. Not that I know anything, but you sound like a DJ on a regular radio station. Like the real deal, legit."

"Aw, thanks."

"I'm serious. It's really cool. So, is that what you want to do? After high school and college, I mean?"

I sigh. "That would be a dream. I'm hoping to find a good communications program, but college is expensive, so unless I can get some good scholarships or an internship to get my foot in the door and recommend me..." I trail off, embarrassed.

Way too much personal information, Jasmine.

Wes nods. "That's cool though. That you have something you love and are good at. I have no idea what I'm going to do. College I guess. I mean, I have to. My parents would disown me if I didn't go."

"Where to?"

He rolls his eyes. "They were both Ivy League, so that's their hope, but there's no way in hell. My grades are good, but not Ivy League material. I don't want that anyway. The only thing I ever wanted to do was be a pilot, like in the Air Force. But that's obviously not a possibility thanks to my messed up brain, so I have to find something else. I'll probably do business or something. My dad's a lawyer, and I definitely do not want that. Thing is, my mom doesn't want me to go away. She constantly worries about me, even now. It's pretty annoying."

I stare at my coffee cup and nod.

"Anyway, this is supposed to be coffee and fun, not let's talk about awful crap, so let's go do something else." He balls up his napkin and tosses it, basketball style, into the nearby can.

"Want to go to Banks?" he asks.

"To the *bank*? What kind of non-date is this?"

Wes grins at me. "What do you people do for fun over at Easton? You've never been to the Banks? It's the park along the river. It's part of Mountain View Reservation."

I look at him blankly.

"The river banks," he says. "Get it? Banks."

"Yeah, I get it. Nope never been. What time is it?" I look at my phone. It's getting late. "I have to get home soon, make sure my brother is in bed and everything," I say. A disturbed night of sleep can bring on seizures for Danny in the worst way. And if Mom kept drinking?

I have to get home.

"Rain check?"

My brows raise. "Confident, are you?"

When his grin widens, I laugh. "We'll see," I answer.

He swings his keys on his finger. "Let me walk you to your car, at least?"

"Fair enough."

On the way to Mom's car, Wes's beeps his key fob in front of a really fancy silver SUV. He opens the door and drops the bag of extra cookies on the leather seat.

"Nice car," I say as he closes the door.

Wes shrugs and looks sheepish. "My parents got it for me."

Oh. Wow. Must be nice. But I don't say anything, my lips so tight they could be sewn together. I'm lucky my mom even let me borrow her piece of crap car. I can't imagine having my own, let alone one like that.

Wes shoves his hands in his pockets as we cross the parking lot toward my car. "Yeah. She always thought I'd never get to drive because of the epilepsy. So when I got the all clear to get my license since my seizures are under control, she was so happy."

"Hmm. That's great, though." I can't imagine the relief of no more seizures. A kernel of hope starts to blossom in my chest, for Danny.

"Yeah, my mom is pretty cool but she likes to show she cares with material things. Money fixes all in the McEnroe house."

"Oh." Okay, so I sound like a moron, but I don't even know how to respond to that. *My mom throws money at problems too. She usually buys herself a bottle of booze when she gets good tips to make her problems go away?* Yeah. I don't think so.

I bite my lip as we cross the parking lot.

"This is me," I say, fishing Mom's keys from my purse. I unlock the door and plop into the driver's seat.

Wes rests his hands on the roof of the car, leaning into the open space. His tee shirt hangs away from his body and rustles in the breeze. My pulse jumps when he leans forward, tanned arms stretched above him, and gives me that smile-smirk of his. "So, when can I see you again?"

My pulse thrums in my ears, my heart yelling *danger*. He's a nice guy and everything, but my recent track record proves I'm not always the best judge of boys' character.

"I mean, for a friendly hike, to the trail at Banks I was telling you about," he talks quickly and I smile to myself. He's nervous.

"We'll see," I say. "For all I know you're some comic book-loving serial killer who plans to take me out in the woods and kill me."

Wes frowns. "Crap. I'm *that* transparent?" He flips his hair back and runs a hand down his face. "Guess I may as well change plans now."

I laugh and shake my head. "There are no plans," I say. "And I really have to get home now."

9

I POP OUT of bed half an hour before my alarm goes off. The Easton Easy Mornings show may not be the Get Up and Go show, but who knows. Maybe it's a step in that direction. I shower and get dressed, taking the time to blow my hair out straight, which is no easy feat. My makeup is on and I'm ready to go before anyone in my house is even awake.

I work quickly in the kitchen, getting Danny's breakfast ready and packing his lunch. I bring his medicine to him and wake him up gently.

"Danny," I whisper. "I have to go to school early to do something. Can you get yourself dressed? Here's your medicine."

He sits up, disoriented.

"I don't want to do school today," he whines, trying to flop back against his pillow. I hold him upright with one hand and wait for him to wake enough to take his meds.

He finally blinks a few times, smiling a sleepy half grin when he focuses on me. "Hi Jazzy."

"Hey kiddo. Here you go." He takes his medicine and I sit on the edge of the bed, watching him as he lies back on his pillow, yawning and stretching and looking at the ceiling.

"So you'll get up and get ready?" I ask again.

"Yes!" He nearly shouts, but he turns over and pulls his iron man comforter back over his head. I sigh. He's not always the easiest to wake up and I don't have time to fight with him today. I look at his bedside clock and debate. I have to get to school.

Pulling his comforter off his head, and making sure to turn his overhead light on, I cross my fingers that he'll get up in time.

"Thanks." I bend to kiss his forehead. "Summer is almost here and then no more early mornings."

Danny groans and rolls over, blinking against the bright light. I stop in his doorway and give him one more glance. He looks okay and I say a silent prayer that the new medicine dose will keep any seizures from breaking through.

He yawns as he sits up. "Where are my shorts? I didn't have any yesterday."

"Hang on," I say, going into the living room for the basket of laundry I folded earlier in the week. I bring him a pair of camo shorts. Danny smiles, the morning crankiness finally ebbing.

"Thanks, Jazzy. Snuggles?" He nestles into my side for a hug and I squeeze him tight, bringing my gaze to his level. "I have to go, okay? I'll wake Mom, but make sure to eat your breakfast and keep on her to get up and get you to the bus stop, okay?"

He nods as I kiss his forehead one more time and go off to wake my mom. I slip out of the house only a few minutes later. Emotions tumble in my stomach, the flip flop of the excited rush I get right before a radio show, and the worry and guilt that I'm not home to make sure Danny's morning goes smoothly.

"GOOD MORNING, EASTON High!" I pull the microphone toward me, feeling the full joy of my voice going out across the airwaves. All my worries fade into the background.

"Today is dedicated to friends, new and old. Write to me at Eastonmornings at Easton dot edu and tell me a friendship story. Who is your best friend? New friend? Old? What has a friend recently done for you that made you realize how awesome they are? I for one, have the absolute best friend a girl can have. She taught me to tie my shoes back in first grade and taught me to parallel park a car just a few months ago. Amazing how many times she's given me a shoulder to cry on and an ear to listen, and she's the absolute funniest person I know. So tell me, listeners, about your friendships—new, old, good or bad, send your stories in! In the meantime, here's a song or two as you all get this amazing day started."

I hit play, setting the shuffle to a few pop songs. I sit back with a smile and wait for the emails to come in. In the meantime, I'll make sure Mom is up and Danny is ready.

My mom rarely answers her cell, so when her voicemail picks up, it's no surprise. I tap the edge of the desk. We had the landline disconnected last year once she got me a cell and put us on a family plan. So it's cell or nothing. I try again and get voicemail yet again. I hope this means she is actually getting ready or already at the bus stop with Danny, and not that she's still in bed. Momentary panic grabs at me. What if something's wrong? What if Danny isn't okay?

But my playlist ends and I pull the mic to me, banishing any other thoughts from interrupting my broadcast.

"This next song is dedicated to Sunita," I say, reading one of the emails in my inbox. "For all the times you listened and cared and are always, always there. Love you! From Shelby. What an awesome dedication. Nothing like a best friend!" I hit play on the next song and sit back again.

My text dings. It's Frankie.

Great show this morning! Love you, bff!

I smile and text back, then scan the emails for what I'll use in my next bit.

An email from Wes McEnroe cycles into the list and I can't help but smile. *How about a song for my new, and kind of dorky, friend?*

Dedicated to her time in the magazine aisle, the subject reads. And in the body of the email a song title:

Free FALLING by Tom Petty. (In case you thought I didn't notice you almost topple over).

Very funny. Falling, eh? Well I'll take your fall and raise you. Two can play at this game. I giggle as I scroll through my music.

I cue up a song and pull the microphone to me. "This next one goes out to someone named Sunny. This listener looks up to Sunny with great admiration, and he admits, sometimes even jealousy for how perfect she truly is as he wishes he could be more like her every day and in every way. So, Sunny, this one is for you. It's an oldie, but here is: "Wind Beneath My Wings.""

I laugh to myself as I play the song, and slide my cell phone toward me. As I expect, it buzzes almost instantly.

OMG. wind beneath my f-n wings?
hahahahhaaa
keep laughing sunny. just wait

I finish my show, turn the recording off, and pack up to get to first period. My program went 45 minutes and I had a lot of segments with friendship dedications and even an on-air caller with a story to share. Next Wednesday I have an interview set up with Student Government Association president Farrah Wiggins, since everyone is dying to know what next year's budget is keeping and cutting as far as extracurriculars and specials. I really need to start prepping for it and nail down my exact questions. I'm obviously trying to get enough clips for my interview to show I know my way around a radio show and on-air interviews are a big part of that. Not that the internship will be much more than probably getting coffee and buttering bagels. Even still, I'd give my left arm to butter bagels for the Get Up and Go crew.

When I close the station door behind me, the energy of my broadcast still pulses through me as I hike my bag on my shoulders and head to first period.

"Jazz!"

My mood plummets faster than a brick dropped in water. I take a deep breath and turn around with a smile for my ex-boyfriend. "What brings you to this far corner of the school, Sebastian? I hope you didn't come all the way over here just to talk to me. Surely you have more important before-school activities to keep you busy? What's her name again?"

I walk fast, fast enough that he has to rush to keep up. "Jazz. Stop walking for a second. Geez, girl."

I stop and cross my arms. "Speak."

"Your show was great this morning."

I compose my face into the coolest expression I can as if I'm utterly bored, even though my heart and thoughts are doing their coyote chasing the roadrunner thing. I shake my head and mentally slap myself. Why am I stopping for him?

Newsflash: I'm not.

"If you've got something to say, Sebastian, spit it out because I have to get to class and I don't have time for this. Or you."

"You seem really good," he says quietly. "Happy."

I don't answer, but inside I seethe. What, does he want me to fall at his feet sobbing and begging for answers on why he threw our relationship away and cheated on me? What the hell? It's like my not falling apart or being outwardly miserable is a disappointment to him or something. I guess my stony exterior is believable after all.

"I mean, I'm happy you're okay."

Maybe it's a guilty conscience. Maybe he's looking to be forgiven. Whatever it is, I'm not taking the bait. *Do not notice how sincere he looks. How sincere he sounds.* I start walking again, more quickly this time, and damn him, he follows me all the way to the science wing.

When I reach my chemistry lab, Sebastian stops me with a hand on my arm before I can escape inside.

"Say something." His eyes search mine and I slap the teeny tiny part of me that knows that look so well and that's tempted by the familiarity.

"What is there to say?" It comes out with way more venom than I intend and Sebastian steps back.

"I'm sorry, okay?" He says the words softly. His hand inches toward mine, and I cross my arms again.

"Yep. *That* I can agree with."

"It was a mistake, Jazz. A huge mistake. I loved you so much. Love you. Please believe me. Give me another chance?"

I take a deep breath. How easy it would be. Too fall back into step with him. To be the other half of Jasmine and Sebastian like I've been for so long.

No way. I can't. I'm worth more than he gave me.

"Sorry Sebastian. You made your decision. We're over. Now please leave me alone."

So I can finish getting over you, once and for all.

Once I'm parked safely at my lab table and away from Sebastian, I pull out my chem book and last week's lab notes with shaking hands. How dare he follow me down here and *apologize* and ruin an otherwise perfectly good day.

I pull out my schedule for next week's Easy Easton Mornings. Going over the details for my interview and segments calms me immediately. By the time Frankie slides into the seat next to mine, I'm feeling totally zen and have almost forgotten about my jackass of an ex.

"You were awesome this morning!" Frankie says. "We were totally listening to you while we had breakfast. Mom says your radio personality is shining through big time."

I smile. Frankie's family has been like a second family to me so many times. Her mom often sends me home with trays of home cooked meals for my family and I always go back-to-school shopping with them, where she manages to buy me a few things. Not to mention listening to my family rants and always giving helpful advice. I seriously love those people.

I whisper-tell Frankie about Sebastian harassing me on the way to class with his weird intentions and apologies. She rolls her eyes but her nostrils flare as she listens to the story.

"What an assclown!" she whispers as our strict chemistry teacher stands in front of the class to begin. "He better stay away from you. You don't need his crap! I'll seriously go off on him, if you want."

"Not worth your time. Or mine."

"He's not getting to you, is he? I mean, not in a take him back sort of way?"

"No way I'll take him back."

Frankie frowns, seeing right to the heart of my emotions. "I know it hurts," she says. "I could kill him for that."

"It's fine," I say. "It's already way better than it was. I just never want to go through this again."

The loudspeaker crackles. "Mr. Karns, can you please send Jasmine Torres down to the office?"

What now? I start to repack my bag, a pit of worry spreading in my stomach like spilled poison. Please, please, please, do not be something serious.

Frankie leans over and whispers.

"Maybe Sebastian is down there crying from his broken heart and they want you to see his anguish?"

I laugh weakly as I pack up and head toward the door.

I move quickly in the hallway though. I get called to the office a lot—it's usually Mom with some message or needing me to do something for Danny or something. We aren't allowed to use cell phones in school so she always calls the main office or guidance, calling me out of class and making a way bigger deal than things need to be. Except of course when it is serious, which happens way too often. But I guess I could be in some kind of trouble. Doubtful, but you never know. Maybe someone caught on to my on the air public insult to Sebastian?

Good morning Easton high, welcome to Today in Jasmine's frantic brain.

Mrs. Robin, the school secretary, stands at the counter collating papers but stops when I come in. She rushes around the counter with a serious look on her face. "Your mom called. There's been a family emergency with your brother. She wanted you to know. She's on her way to the hospital and said she'll call you when she has more news."

I fall into one of the office waiting room chairs. Damn it. I squeeze my eyes shut. When I open them the room appears tilted and my breath comes in short bursts. "It was another seizure."

Mrs. Robin sits next to me with a hand on my knee. "I'm sorry sweetie. It was. She said it happened at school. She'll call you as soon as she has news."

"I need to get there."

Mrs. Robin nods. "Do you have a car? I'm sure Dr. Johnson would excuse the day given the circumstances."

I shake my head, my face buried in my hands. I thought he was better now. I thought the new medicine would help. It's only been a few weeks, but we were all starting to let our guard down. I take short, rapid-fire, machine gun breaths.

"How about another family member?" Mrs. Robin asks. But we've been through this before. There is no one else in my family that can help. But I guess they have to ask.

I look at her, but everything is blurry, as if she's under water. "Frankie. Her mom gave permission for her to help out when needed," I say. "She's my best friend."

Mrs. Robin gently takes my hand and leads me to the principal's office. "Let's go talk to Dr. Johnson and see if we can work this out to get you to your family."

10

FRANKIE DRIVES TO the hospital with one hand on mine. I lean my head back against the seat, trying to calm my racing mind. Frankie's citrusy perfume fills the space and every deep breath I take is filled with it. It's familiar and comforting, even though it's strong enough to make my eyes water.

I just hung up with Mom. She's still at the hospital, but it seems Danny is stable. Apparently, it wasn't too bad, all things considered, but since the school's policy is to always call the ambulance when there is a seizure, a trip to the hospital was in order. But I don't know the details yet so I'm not sure how true that is.

We're silent all the way there, which is welcome. I hate the pity looks people give me when they find out my brother has epilepsy. Or worse, the well-meaning *he'll be okay* statements. I mean, he may not be okay. Ever. I hope he is, but there are no guarantees. Anyway, with Frankie, even as loud as she is, she knows when I need her to just quietly be there.

She pulls into the St. Bonaventure complex and drives toward the parking lot.

"You can drop me off at the door."

"I'm coming in." She says it like she's made a decision. But there's no need. She shouldn't miss school. Frankie is super strict about attendance and grades. I know she wants to be there for me, but it's really not necessary.

"I'm fine. I'd rather deal with my mom alone. Seriously."

"You're sure?"

"I'm sure. Besties?"

"Forever." With a quick hug goodbye, she drops me off, and I walk into the hospital with my heart thumping.

When I get to the pediatric ER, Danny is sitting up on the second bed, reading an obviously well worn (and probably covered in gross germs) copy of an old Dr. Seuss book. Mom sits in a chair against the wall, her face drooping with exhaustion. She gives me a small, weak-tea smile.

"Hey!" I pull Danny into a hug. He smells like Danny, all little boy sweat and dirt with a faint whiff of Doritos, and his arms wrap around me like they always do, little fingers settling softly against the back of my neck. I pull back and look into his eyes. Regular Danny. I exhale. "How you doing, buddy?"

"I'm fine, Jazzy! I only fell asleep. This is stupid I have to be here. We had an assembly this afternoon. With a *hypnotist*. A real live hypnotist! And I am missing it. So why do I have to be here *again*? I'm sick of this. I miss everything." He kicks the book off the side of the bed.

Blowing out a huge breath, I sit next to him and try to pull him closer but he pushes me away.

"Come on, Danny. Tell me what happened."

He shakes his head violently, the wires, electrodes and mesh cap whipping with the movement.

"I'm sick of talking about it. Nothing happened! I told you I was just tired." He crosses his arms and looks up at the television. "Leave me alone!"

Mom raises her eyebrows and gives me a look that says this isn't the first time she's heard Danny say this this morning. I raise mine in return. What do I try next? A little help from her would be nice. Geez.

I decide to take a different approach, sticking with topics that make Danny happy. "Did you draw anything today?"

84

His eyes light up a little. "Yeah. I drew Iron Man at snack time. You can see it later."

"Cool. So what happened after that? After snack?"

He gives me a warning look, but not nearly as volatile as he was a few minutes ago.

"It was in math," he says, brown eyes huge in his face. "After snack I get tired sometimes. It was nothing. I think I fell asleep for a minute. My teacher makes a big deal over everything. And then I look like a big idiot in front of all my friends!"

I sigh, and pick up his hand in mine, kissing his knuckles. There's no way to know what really happened. "I doubt anyone thinks that. Your friends love you. Your teacher is only being careful to take care of you, like she does with everyone in the class."

Mom gives me a low thumbs up for smoothing things over and the iceberg around the Mom part of my heart softens a little. I take in a shaky breath, hoping I made him feel at least a little better about it all.

"Are you tired now?" I ask. "Why don't you rest? You can show me your pictures when you wake up." I lower his bed and tuck the thin blanket around him. I pick up the book from the floor and lay it beside him. "You can keep looking at this or watching TV, but let's turn off the light. Mom and I will step into the hall, okay? We'll be right there so just call out if you need us."

He flips onto his side and glances up at the TV playing cartoons on mute. I check the video monitor to make sure it's on and motion to the hallway, slipping into one of the plastic chairs just outside Danny's curtained room.

"So what happened?" I don't mean it in a confrontational way at all, even though when I talk to Mom my voice tends to take on that tone.

"His teacher said he was staring for a long time."

"Wait, what? You're having them do all this for an absence seizure? So he gets put through all this for nothing?"

But she crosses her arms and stands in front of me. She's not in the mood to back down today either.

"I'm not a total idiot, Jasmine. He was unresponsive, even after being carried to the nurse. And he was still completely limp. The doctor said it sounds like one of his complex partials." She sinks into the chair beside mine.

"Crap." I knew a basically benign (for Danny) absence seizure was too good to be true. My mom covers her face with her hands and damnit if I don't actually feel—okay fine, only a little, but still—bad for her.

"Sorry mom," I say. "I didn't mean it like that. I don't think you're an idiot." (White lies are okay when people are crying). "I'm just stressed."

"I know, me too. When does it get better for him, you know?" She sighs.

"Yep."

"Plus, I have no idea how we're going to pay for yet another hospital visit. With our insurance being as crappy as it is, who knows how much this is going to cost us."

I literally have to bite my tongue. Yeah, I get it, we have no money. But who thinks of that when their kid is in the hospital? Maybe if she'd sell that stupid expensive collector's stereo dad left behind, instead of hanging onto it like he's coming back, she could pay for some stuff. But that's an argument we've had way too many times to bring up now.

I stand and peek in Danny's room. "Asleep," I say. "I'm going to run to the vending machine. Be right back. Want anything?"

Mom dismisses me with a shake of her head. The second I walk down the hall I feel better. I know it's awful, but I can't help it. Being near her drives me crazy.

I get a bag of cheese doodles, a bag of peanut M&Ms and a bottle of water. What can I say? I'm a stress eater. I drop onto the couch next to the vending machine and pull out my phone. Almost lunch time already? Wow. Hospital time is some weird time suck vortex. I text Wes.

guess where I am?

Wes is at school, obviously, but he'll get my text eventually.

sunny!

His answer is almost immediate and I can't help but smile.

no idea. um, waiting somewhere for me to passionately make out with you?
um, hello... friends!
right. So... I give up?
st. bonaventure.
shit.
yeah.
danny?
yep. complex partial.
that sucks. been there. he okay?
i think so.
you okay?
i think so.
want me to come hang out with you? i have like, permanent medical excuses. i prefer to use them for the beach and stuff, but i can take one for the team.
har har
seriously though.

we r fine. hopefully we'll go home soon. mom says they aren't admitting him. of course she's also too busy complaining about hospital costs. she makes me crazy.

I immediately regret telling him too much about money complaints. Him with the brand new luxury car and material payoffs from his parents.

you sure? i'm about to go into AP physics. i would love to use you as an excuse to get out of that. i mean, i would love to be there for you.
AP? oooh, you're fancy. no. we're fine.
okay then. talk later?

I don't answer. What does that mean? Text? It can't mean call, right?
My phone dings while I'm trying to figure out what to say.

i mean to let me know how he is.

Phew. Awkwardness avoided.

sure.
tomorrow. plans?

I debate again but then type.

depends on danny. y?
if all is well want to hang out?
doing?
;)
OMG please don't be a perv. i thought you were a nice guy.

aw, you think I'm nice.

anyway.

to banks, remember? there's this cool hiking trail. it's awesome.

sounds good. but I have to work on my interview. it's important.

bring it. can i help?

I smile at the suggestion. Hanging with Wes may be the perfect distraction.

if danny is better, then yes.

sweet. wear good hiking shoes. and give me your address. i'll pick you up.

you sure?

yeah. can i meet your mom?

not unless you want to risk catching rabies.

harsh.

txt you later?

yep.

I tuck my phone into my back pocket and finish my snacks. I look longingly at the pretzel sticks and granola bars, but I've met my calorie and sodium content for the rest of the week with the junk I've already consumed. I stand and trudge back toward Danny's room, hoping he gets to go home to his normal life soon.

11

WHEN WES AND I get to the hiking trail, I can hardly believe how peaceful it is. Everything is so green and lush and… quiet. I'm instantly grateful I didn't back out at the last minute, tempting as it was. Mom, Danny and I got home from the hospital super late last night, but luckily they released him with a pretty decent EEG report and nothing more than yet another minor medication change. Even still, the exhaustion this morning had almost made me miss this.

I follow Wes up a relatively steep trail. It's crazy beautiful with streams and waterfalls and a canopy of thick oaks. It's a hot day, but relatively cooler under the trees. Tree roots crisscross beneath our feet and I brace my sneakers against the thicker ones for leverage. In some places the path is incredibly narrow, walled in by large rocks on either side. I put my palm against them as I pass, loving the feel of the cool stone beneath my hand. The climb is far from treacherous, but it takes effort and my breathing comes quick and uneven on the climb. The higher we get, the freer I feel. The air gets thinner as we climb but I take big gulps of it as if it's the first breath I'm ever taking.

The further we go, the more the stress of my life drops away. All of it—school and home and Danny and internships and Mom and scholarships—has been wound so tightly around me like a rope that kept me from breathing. But as we make our way up that mountain trail, it's like that rope of worries loosens and falls away.

We reach the pinnacle of the small mountain in less than an hour. We aren't all that high, but even still, I've never seen my town like this. Simply amazing. Beautiful.

Wes plops down on a flat rock and drops his bag beside him, rustling around inside it. As I sit down beside him, he pulls out a knife.

"I knew it," I deadpan. "You're a murderer."

He takes an apple out of the bag and rolls his eyes. "I see the other part of that thought in your eyes," he says with a grin as he slices the apple. *"I knew he was too good to be true."*

"Oh God, ego much?" I laugh as I take the slice of apple he offers. "It's so beautiful up here. I can't believe I never knew this existed."

"Yeah. It's my favorite hike. I don't come all that much, because it's a dicey trek alone."

"I love it." I look out over the town, way down below. "I feel so small up here. Or maybe it's all that down there that's small. I don't know, but it's perfect."

Wes nods, chewing. "That's my favorite part." He stares off as if deep in thought. I find myself scanning the streets and trees below, wondering about all the busy, individual lives. All the different problems.

"So," he says. "What's with that interview thing you were talking about?"

I take a deep breath and feel instantly filled with excitement. "It's an on-air interview. We've had a ton of budget cuts at Easton in the last few years. It's honestly a miracle we still have the radio station, but Ms. Hudson fights hard and I bet puts in a bunch of her own money to keep us going. Anyway, student government has been working with the PTA and Board of Ed to figure out which programs stay, which programs go, what we need to do as a school to keep what we want, and all that. So I'm interviewing this girl Farrah, the president of the SGA to talk about it all. I know it probably sounds boring, but at our school, people are really worried they're going to lose their particular extracurriculars."

"That sucks. So, you want to practice your questions on me? I do an awesome student government impersonation." He tosses a piece of apple in the air and catches it in his mouth.

I laugh. "I haven't written them yet. Thanks to last night's later than expected St. Bonaventure adventure, I have nothing to practice. Tomorrow, though. I *have* to get this done."

Wes nods and squints into the sun overhead.

Not that I want to compare because that is a dangerous game that has the potential to put you on the fast track to crazytown, but Sebastian had never and would never give a crap about my radio work. I try to imagine him offering to help me prep an interview. Would never happen.

I push Sebastian's name and face as far from my mind as possible, mentally throwing the whole relationship over the side of this cliff. It's a weird moment, like I'm being reborn up here, leaving everything behind that I don't want or need, or tossing it off the mountain and letting it fly away. I close my eyes and turn my face to the sun. The peace of the woods and the quiet and the warmth lull me into a sort of forced meditation. When I open my eyes, spots dance in my vision and the light touches everything differently than when I last looked. Wes stares at me with a tiny smile.

I slide my sunglasses back down over my eyes. "What?"

"You looked so peaceful."

"Completely," I say.

"That's why I love it up here," he says. "It's just… free. No expectations."

"Yep. No problems or responsibilities."

After a few more minutes of silence and peace, Wes stands up, extending a hand to help me to my feet. His light hair hangs in his eyes and he sweeps it back with his other hand. When he pulls me up I stand a little too close to him for a beat too long before turning toward the path.

He sighs as we start to make our way down the trail. "I don't suppose you would tell me what you were thinking about up there, huh?"

"Not a chance." I follow his footfalls down the path. It gets rocky in places and I reach a hand out against the passing tree trunks to keep my balance.

"How about this?" Wes is out of breath, but his voice still carries that childish la-dee-da of mischief. "I'll tell you one of my deep dark secrets and you tell me one of yours."

I keep walking down the steep path. I don't even know how to respond to that.

"Okay," he says. "This is horrifically embarrassing and I've never told a soul. Ready?"

"Hmmm."

"I broke my arm when I was ten years old. I was on the roof pretending to fly a plane and fell off."

"Oh my God! You're lucky you didn't break your head open."

He laughs. "My parents freaked out. It was summer so the whole neighborhood was practically outside. It was very dramatic. But I've wanted to fly a plane since I can remember and that valley where our two roofs meet always looked like a cockpit to my ten-year-old eyes. I couldn't help myself. Your turn."

I consider how to answer as I follow closely behind him.

"No one knows this." I say this in an ominous way as if I'm spilling the deepest of dark secrets. I pause for dramatic effect. "But black jellybeans are my favorite flavor."

Wes stops and turns around, his face all mock horror as if I told him I'd once killed someone. "Ew! Who likes black jelly-beans?"

"Exactly." I hang my head in shame. "Hence the secrecy."

His, much-as-I-hate-to-admit-it, adorable smirk pops up.

"Next confession," he says, turning back to the path. "My first seizure was when I was five years old. I spent most of that year in the hospital and had to repeat kindergarten."

My heart dips, imagining him young and vulnerable. Just like Danny. I watch him climb down the path in front of me. He's on the thin side, but agile, vulnerable but confident. I can only hope for the same for my brother.

"When did you get them under control?" I ask softly.

"By seven or so? The medicines can sometimes be a bitch though. But they work. I've had some breakthrough seizures, especially in middle school. But nothing else in years. I go in once in a while now for tests, like when I met you, but that's it."

"That's awesome." And I mean it too. The thought that he can live with this, successfully, happily, normal. Ordinary. My heart squeezes with hope for my brother.

"Your turn."

How do I follow that confession? What can I reveal about myself? His confession definitely deserves something honest.

I take a deep breath. "I caught my boyfriend cheating on me. Like literally walked in on him. Them. Really recently. So we broke up." I feel stupid when I say it, but well, there the words go, filling up the air just like the sunshine waltzing down through the break in oak leaves overhead.

"Ouch."

"Yeah. Total asshole. Obviously."

"Sounds like a complete idiot to me. To cheat on a girl like you."

I shrug, ignoring the burn in my cheeks.

"How long did you guys go out?"

"Almost a year? I don't know. Too long. Waste of my time."

My mouth goes totally dry. Talking about Sebastian was a bad idea. I reach around into my backpack to get my water. My foot slips with the shift and I cringe, arms flailing as I try and grab onto something so I won't hit the ground.

"Oomph." I land with a soft thud and blink into Wes's blue eyes, which are about one inch from mine. He wiggles beneath me and I realize he broke my fall. His body is warm against mine, his heavy cotton cargo shorts scratchy on my skin. Damn my short shorts.

And now, listeners, let's share some of the most mortifyingly awkward situations in our lives!

"I'm so sorry." I squirm off him and try to stand. The steep incline only makes me lose my balance again and I tip forward, grabbing his shoulder for balance. I land on him again, practically straddling him this time.

Awesome. Kill me now.

I scramble off him, sitting on the ground beside him and wishing I could fall straight into the center of the earth.

Wes laughs as he grabs my hands tightly in his. He means to help me up, I know, but his thumbs brush across my knuckles. And his eyes never leave mine.

"Most awkward non-date ever?" I say to break the silence.

"Yeah." He stands up and, still holding my hands, helps me up. "About that…"

Our hands are still clasped between us, his gaze dropping down to my lips.

What is my brain thinking? Or not thinking? I drop my hands and move to continue on the path. But Wes blocks the way and won't move. Even when I try and shoulder past him.

"Seriously," he says quietly. "Why?"

"Why what?" I dig in my bag for the water bottle that caused me to lose my balance in the first place. My mouth is all Sahara desert and besides, I don't want to talk about it.

His hand on my arm stops my rustling and when I look up, he's still staring at me.

"Come on," he says. "Let me take you on a non non-date."

"No." Screw the water. This whole thing was a mistake. I'm not ready for this. I zip my bag and push around him. The trail levels out and I pick up speed. His footsteps soon fall in step with mine, beside me. Infuriating.

"What if it's a really bad date?"

"Nope."

"If I make it terrible, it will hardly count as a date at all, really."

I walk faster.

"You can pay for yourself! Hell, you can even pay for me, if you want. It will be the non datiest date ever."

I shake my head.

"What restaurant do you hate? I'll take you there."

My lips betray me by twitching into a smile. Thankfully he's behind me and can't see.

"We'll even sit at different tables. You can pretend you don't know me."

Giggles start to bubble up my throat, like some elementary school volcano science project.

"You just don't give up, do you?" I say, out of breath. I turn around with my hands on my hips.

He trots up beside me, all smiling and disheveled from our trek and, thanks to me, tumble on the trail.

"I'm feeling a little hopeful," he says. "Is that what I should be feeling?"

I start down the trail again, more slowly this time. "I'm not going out to dinner," I say.

"Breakfast? Lunch?"

"No. A meal is definitely a date. And don't even *think* about suggesting a movie."

He hands me his canteen and I stop to drink the cool water. Instant relief. Never mind that my lips are touching where his lips just were.

"Next weekend," he says. "How about Saturday? I'll come up with the worst plan ever. I promise."

12

I SPEND ALL of Sunday working on my interview questions, doing homework, and hanging out with Danny. Mom is working a double shift at the bar, which hopefully means buying Danny's medicines this month will be easier to afford. Not to sound like her, but the hospital bills will be rolling in soon and that means she will be tearing her hair out and freaking out about how to pay for them. Even with insurance, there is always so much to pay for, and for her to stress about and drink over. I haven't even been for a checkup in three years, to try and save money. Not that she told me not to go. I just stopped making my appointments. In the world of Elena, kids do for themselves as soon as they can. She sure as hell isn't going to remember to make something as simple as a checkup appointment for me.

I think that's why Danny's illness turned her even worse than she used to be. She had all this added pressure to start doing extra stuff for him, being a mom, showing up places and taking care of him. She did it for a while, and a decent job at it, too. But then it was all too much for her to handle, so as soon as I could step in and pick up the slack, I did. Thankfully I'm a lot older than him. When Danny got sick, Mom's drinking, which started to be a problem back when Dad left, turned into Mom passed out on the couch pretty much every single freaking day.

And today listeners, let's talk about Jasmine's pathetic life! Up next: how to fool the world into thinking your family is normal to avoid being reported to child services.

I sigh. Danny is getting better. If we can get his seizures under control and keep them that way, that's all that matters. Even if Mom is messed up, Danny has me. But what if he doesn't get better? What if he gets worse?

I think about Wes. How confident he is, how he seems to have a perfectly normal life doing normal high school stuff. Why can't Danny have that same bright future? Another tiny kernel of hope blossoms.

I think about Wes and my non non-date next weekend and wonder what terrible idea he'll come up with for us.

I know it's too soon to look forward to hanging out with a boy, but the admission whispers through me that I really am. It doesn't have to mean anything, anyway. He's a friend, who happens to be a boy. A cute boy. A very sweet, funny and witty boy.

Oh my God, Jasmine you are actually listing his good attributes. You need to chill.

And you actually used the word witty.

Anyway, it's not a real date. I'm not ready for something like that. But I'm allowed to have fun with someone who makes me laugh.

End of story.

My cell phone rings, pulling me out of my daydream. Good thing too, because I need to get back to work.

Sebastian.

Oh, hell no.

Just what I need. I send it to voicemail and go back to my chemistry text book. Two minutes later my text dings. Of course my ex-boyfriend will not leave me alone. Ugh. Come on, universe, can't you make him go away?

jazz, i need to talk to u. IMPORTANT.

I frown at the screen. Sebastian is many things—I stop my mind before it launches into a tirade of expletives—but he doesn't often tend to be overdramatic. So now I wonder if something really *is* wrong. I mean, yeah, I know what he did to me is horrible, but even still, I should make sure everything's okay.

My insides clench as, despite my better judgment, I call him back.

"Are you okay?" I ask as soon as he picks up.

"Of course." He has the audacity to sound smug which lights a fire inside me.

"Jazz," I recite from his text. "I need to talk to you. Important! Important? What the hell, Seb? What's so important?"

"I wanted to know if you had what you needed for our English presentation tomorrow."

I could punch something. Instead, I force a fake laugh. "*That's* why you called me?"

"What?" he huffs. "Just because you hate me is no reason for us to get a bad grade. You didn't even bother to come to school on Friday, so I wasn't sure if you were caught up."

"Didn't bother? Screw you, Sebastian. Danny was in the hospital again. And anyway, Trina emailed me the part of the presentation I'm responsible for. Don't worry, I'll be ready."

"Shit. I didn't know. I'm sorry. Is he okay?"

"Like you care." It's a low blow, but I can't help it. I want him completely out of my life.

He sighs on the other end of the line. "Is this the way it's going to be?"

"Do you think you deserve anything less?"

"Maybe not. But seriously, is he okay? You may not believe it, but I do still care about you. And your family."

"He's fine." I ignore the stirring in my stomach. Sebastian is most definitely not worth even a second of my time, or any of my emotions. I can't let him weasel his way back in.

"That's good. So… what's up with you? You seem so happy."

This again?

Silence. As awkward as dead radio air.

Sebastian clears his throat. "I have to ask. Did you meet someone?"

"Did I *meet* someone? You are such a piece of work, Sebastian. And a piece of something else, too."

If internal organs could seethe, every single one of mine would be doing exactly that. I resent the hell out of Sebastian's nerve, but there's also a tiny part of me that wants to see him squirm.

"So what if I did?" I say coolly. "Meet someone. What's it to you?"

More silence.

Sweet, heavenly, in-your-face silence.

Yes, I realize how awful, immature, and ridiculous this tactic makes me. No, at this moment, I don't care.

"I don't get it," he sputters. "We broke up, what, not even a month ago. How could you possibly meet someone already?"

"So says he who met someone *before* said breakup?"

He's quiet and I imagine there is a good bit of seething happening on his end too. I'd be lying if I said it didn't feel good.

"Probably not a good idea if we talk," I say. "No hard feelings or anything. I just don't need the drama."

"You mean your new boyfriend doesn't want you talking to me."

My fingers flex. Man, I'd love to slap him.

"First of all, I don't have a boyfriend. Second of all, no one tells me what to do or who to talk to. You of all people should know that, Seb. The only person who doesn't want me talking to you, is me. So drop dead."

I hit the end button with a flourish as if I'm banishing Seb to outer space for the rest of his days.

Broadcast over.

I flop down on my bed, massaging my temples and trying like anything to clear my mind and settle the storm inside me. Sebastian is so not worth this. I push aside my chem textbook and pull out Farah's interview questions.

So.

Concentration.

I work on my questions solemnly, trying to forget my conversation with Sebastian. Fine. I shouldn't have let him believe I had a new guy already. But he shouldn't have called me either. I'm moving on, and doing a damn good job of it, too, considering how bad he hurt me. Sure, I still miss him a lot of days, and yeah, I still ache with what was and could have been. But he doesn't get the right to try to get to me and mess up my progress.

At least an hour passes as I work quietly, fine tuning each question and making a list of possible answers to segue between topics. Reading over them again, I feel pretty confident about it all. When I'm done, I pull out my English book, along with the questions Trina sent me for our stupid presentation.

I'm nearly done with my homework when my phone dings with a text. I cringe, hoping against all hope that it is *not* Sebastian. I'm in luck. It's not. And even better, it's Wes.

Ready to practice your interview yet?

Funny you should ask. I type. I just finished the questions.

13

I SLEEP LIKE a rock Sunday night, which is pretty shocking considering what an insane week this is going to be. When I wake up on Monday, I feel like a soldier prepared for battle. All my plans in place, I walk into school feeling more than confident. I practically float down the hallway. My radio show goes perfectly and I smile, knowing I have another good segment recorded for our NYC meeting next week. I hurry from the room to get to chemistry in time.

When I see Sebastian standing at my locker, I turn and walk the other way. I'd rather carry all my heavy books to first period than have him try to ruin my perfect mood.

Determination.

I practice my English presentation at lunch for Frankie.

"You are so going to rock it," she says, twirling her fork through her salad like she wishes it was spaghetti.

"Want to do something after school?" I ask. I miss my silly afternoons with Frankie where we do homework, sing around our houses like rock stars, read out loud from our favorite magazines, eat gooey bad-for-you snacks or do fashion shows in each other's clothes to try to spruce up our wardrobes.

"Yes!" she says. "Can we get froyo on the way home?"

"Of course. Let's go to my house though. I want to be there when Danny gets home."

We continue through the rest of lunch with plans while I quietly wait for the day to tick to its end. I don't even mind class presentations, but doing one with Sebastian, though thankfully we have Trina to keep us from committing murder in front of the entire junior year English class, is not something I'm looking forward to.

After my telling him to drop dead on the phone and avoiding him at every turn today, I was sure Sebastian would be seething mad. But, his face is blank when we arrive in English and he reads through his cards like a robot. He goes out of his way to not look at me and even though we're standing next to each other at the front of the room, he pulls into himself, arms at his sides, as if he's afraid we'll bump hands accidentally or something.

He's totally uncomfortable around me. Good. It's about time.

Trina reads nervously through her part, but she smiles a lot and makes eye contact and her information is all correct.

When it's my turn, I take a step forward and deliver my planned presentation flawlessly. I let my eyes roam across the room to each person, stopping at Mr. James as I deliver most of the speech. I'm not in love with public speaking, but I pretend I'm on the air instead of in front of a room full of people. Plus, having Sebastian in my group is added motivation. I want him to see how good I'm doing. How in control I am. See who doesn't need you, sucker?

When the final bell rings I shoot from the room, with no chance whatsoever of having to interact with my ex-boyfriend.

how did it go? Wes's text comes almost the second the final bell of the day buzzes. The faintest flutters rise in my chest.

awesome. not that I was worried.

ur confidence is adorable. I could just kiss you..... so you know.

104

ha! there will be none of that. not if you were the last living guy on earth. :)

we'll see. u may be surprised at how awful of a time i'll give you. you'll fall madly in love with me... i can see it now....

I roll my eyes and drop my phone into my purse, my lips tugging up into what I'm sure must be a very broad smile.

THE ENGLISH PRESENTATION may not have had me nervous, but the SGA interview has me more than a little rattled. I head to school Wednesday morning with a tornado twisty feeling in the pit of my stomach. This interview is really important, obviously. I mean, most of Easton will probably be listening to see where things stand. But, it's also going to be the only interview in my submission package for the WYN60 internship. So it needs to be solid. I practice my questions in my mind on the entire walk to school, using my internal radio voice the whole way.

Good morning Easton High! Today we're here with Farrah Wiggins, student government president and Board of Ed liaison. Farrah, thank you so much for talking with us today on this very important topic that affects almost all students at Easton in one way or another.

I practice this opening relentlessly on my way to school and by the time I get into the parking lot, a good half an hour before my show even starts, I'm feeling pretty confident. I walk through the quiet halls as if they exist just for me.

"Hi, Mr. Tony." I wave to the janitor.

He gives me a small smile and nods toward the radio station around the corner. "Good luck today, miss."

Even Mr. Tony knows about the radio show and interview? Wow.

Turning the corner and squinting down the hall, I try to figure out what's in front of the station door. As I get closer, the bright blobs start to take shape.

Flowers? Bright Gerbera daisies, in every color? They're absolutely gorgeous.

I approach them carefully, as if they may be explosive, bending to get the card, hoping they are from anyone but Sebastian. I don't think it would be like him to try and rattle me before my big interview, but I'm positive he wouldn't send me flowers for any authentic reason, either. But who else would?

When I open the card, my eyes scan quickly, and I laugh really loud, right there in the middle of the empty hallway. Then, like some silly girl in a movie or a book, I press the card to my chest and laugh some more.

I hope you like flowers. I called every florist looking for dead ones, because I don't want to give you the wrong idea. But, turns out there is not a big market for dead flowers and they were all out. The nerve! I was short on time or dumpster diving would have been my next course of action. So, hope these will do. Good luck today. Break a leg. Does break a leg apply to radio? Well, break whatever you're supposed to on the radio. You'll do great. I'll be listening. Wes

Wes. I smile and drop my bag, rushing back down the hall to find Mr. Tony. Now I know what that look was about when I passed him. Did Wes have these delivered?

"Mr. Tony!" I call when I see him down the hall. "Did you see who left the flowers?"

He nods as he methodically pushes and pulls his mop back and forth across the floor. "Was a young man," he says. "Asked right where the radio station was that had the best high school DJ in New Jersey."

"Thanks!" I turn and rush back toward the station, shaking my head. I can't believe Wes actually came here himself this early in the morning.

ur the best. I text him. thank you.

Wes doesn't respond and I can only imagine my compliment has stunned him into a very unusual silence.

I flip on the lights and start to get everything set up for my interview with Farrah Wiggins. The flowers sit between my computer and microphone, making the small room an even brighter spot in my morning. They're only flowers, but my eyes flit to them as I set up my computer and sound check the microphones, when I open my document of questions and test the sound board. They're like an omen or something, a guarantee that the morning will go well.

Farrah arrives about ten minutes before the interview is set to start. Farrah is a senior, but she seems much older. She's poised and incredibly smart, not to mention really nice, too. She glides into the room, her long braids and the beads on the end of them swishing and clicking together.

"Hey!" Farrah slides into the seat across the radio desk with a big smile on her face. Even her overbite doesn't detract from her openly friendly and pretty face. She has two Dunkin' Donuts coffees and bottles of water in a holder and she offers me one of each.

"Awesome, thanks. I'm running on pure adrenalin this morning, so this is amazing." I mix in a few packets of sugar and take a big gulp.

"No problem," Farrah says. "So, I'm kind of a little nervous about this."

"It's nothing, you'll do great. Just imagine when you have the SGA meetings and all those people are watching. It's like that, but easier, because the people aren't even in the room."

She nods.

"So, we'll talk about stuff the SGA is up to. Wrap up of what you guys did this year, upcoming stuff for next. But mostly, we'll focus on the recent meetings with the Board of Ed and any hints or ideas on programs that may not be around next year."

"Alright. Sounds good. There's nothing set in stone yet, so I'm a bit ambivalent about stirring up controversy by mentioning things that may be on the chopping block, but I have no problem discussing the things that have definitely been approved to stay."

"Perfect. Taking a positive look sounds like a good idea. No reason to get people upset for no reason. Just know they will ask or infer after hearing what *is* staying, but we'll field those questions appropriately. Sound good?"

She gulps down her coffee with a smile. "Ready when you are."

I've been on the radio show countless times over the last few years, but whenever I have an interview guest, I get a little shaky, and the fact that this one is going in my internship submission packet makes it even more nerve wracking.

Deep breath. Let's do this.

"Good morning Easton High! Today I have Farrah Wiggins with me here talking about all the completely awesome things the Student Government Association has been doing for our school. Farrah is the Student Government Association president as well as the Board of Ed liaison. Hello Farrah and thanks for coming to talk to us today on these very important topics that affect so many students at Easton."

"Happy to be here," she says with a genuine smile.

We launch into small talk first. Farrah fills everyone in on the upcoming end of year carnival. I smile, thinking of Trina in English and how excited she is about the carnival. I let Farrah go on for a while, thinking all the Trina-type listeners will be squealing with excitement while listening.

"It's going to be the best carnival, yet," Farrah says. "We have a ton of parent volunteers and donations this year. As you know, our budgets have been drastically cut so we were sure the carnival wouldn't happen. But local business donations have almost completely funded the event. There will be food and games stands available for a nominal fee to the patrons, but the Ferris wheel will be free to riders all afternoon thanks to the folks at E&M Hardware, who sponsored the ride. We have even booked some entertainment thanks to local business donations. A local folk band will be performing for most of the afternoon. One of our parents even works over at Anderson's airfield and we're in the process of arranging a possible short airshow, which will be completely donated time by the pilots and airfield staff."

"Very, very cool," I say. "I, for one, cannot wait for the carnival."

Okay, so radio personalities embellish and lie sometimes. All in the name of doing the job.

"Me too," Farah says. But I read her lips instead of hearing her voice in my headphones.

Crap.

I check the wires quickly and see everything's plugged in.

"Thanks so much for sharing that information with us," I say into the mic. But once again, I hear nothing in my headphones. Crap. I'm not sure we're broadcasting.

Farrah's eyes are wide and dart between me and the mic, her mouth drawn in a panicked grimace. I smile to try to calm her, but my palms are slick. I wipe them on my capris as I turn to my monitor. Click, scroll and I get a short playlist going. Music streams through the speakers.

Momentary reprieve, not optimal, but better than dead air.

"Is everything okay?" Farrah's voice pitches with worry as I drop to the floor to fumble with the wires.

"Just a small technical glitch." In actuality, I have no idea what the hell is wrong. I wish Ms. Hudson was here. What if I can't get us back online? What if my interview is totally ruined. What if…

Aha! A wire near the back of the wall isn't plugged in all the way. No, crap, the outlet itself is loose. I push the plug in tighter just as the next song starts. Sweat drips down the back of my neck as I slide out from under the table and into my seat. I slide my headphones on and test the mic.

Nothing. Shit shit shit.

I press my foot against the plugs.

"Shit," I mutter against the mic. This time, the glorious sound of my voice fills my headphones. I give Farrah a thumbs up as I keep my foot positioned on the plug.

Get it together Jasmine. You're a pro, act like it.

Holy sweaty DJ. And my mouth feels like I've swallowed a bag of dust. But my song is ending and here we go!

"Hello Easton High! Hope you enjoyed that brief interlude of the top 40 while Farrah and I got ready for your calls. Let's hear a little more about what Student Government has been working on this year and then we'll take your questions."

Farrah licks her lips and leans into the microphone on her side of the table. With a nervous smile, she launches into all the things SGA has accomplished during this school year, mainly fundraising efforts, social committees and events and community service projects. Her passion for the subject helps her nerves fall away and when I notice she's smiling more and licking her lips less, I decide it's time to change course. And, thank God, the microphone is working fine so far.

"So," I say. "You know the questions the students are really after. Tell us about the budget next year. I'm sure it's not finalized, but can you give us some hints?"

"I'm so happy you asked that! You're right, so much of it isn't finalized yet. And, don't forget, I'm not privy to everything that goes on in those Board of Ed decisions."

"Of course, we realize that. But, come on, give us something. What do we have to worry about getting cut next year?"

Farrah takes a sip of her water. The question has thrown her off. "I'll tell you the things I know have approval, so far, but there really is so much more on the table for them to discuss."

"I hope our little radio station is safe?" I joke, trying to steer her back to a comfortable mood.

Farrah offers a big grin. "Gosh, I sure hope so too! You guys are my favorite way to start the day!"

"Thanks for that," I say. "Now, back on track. What else can we be sure to see around here next year?"

"Like I said, I only know of a few thus far, but that's only because most meetings and decisions will be made over the summer. I do know football, basketball, and baseball will be around next year, as well as art, jazz band and theater."

She spins it in a way that makes it sound like the things not mentioned haven't been discussed yet, but I know grumblings about certain programs have been rumored to be cut. Like golf, lacrosse, marching band and debate team, to name a few. I don't dig deeper, because for all I know these things, and others, do still have a chance to be approved. Like she said, no reason to start any rumors or mass hysteria.

"Let's take a call, shall we?"

"Sure!" Farrah's voice is cheerful but her face is drawn with worry.

The first caller asks questions mostly about the carnival, which Farrah answers cheerfully. Every time we talk into the mic, I cringe, hoping it doesn't go out again. I keep my foot poised on the plug.

"Okay," I say in my smoothest on-air voice. "Let's take another call."

"Sounds great," Farrah answers.

"Good morning, you're live with Jasmine Torres and Farrah Wiggins," I answer.

"Hey there," a male voice says. "I have a question for Farrah."

"Go right ahead," I say. "You're live."

"Do you really think it's fair that something like debate could be cancelled and yet we have some stupid carnival? It's amazing what you people do. Like, only the stuff the popular kids like gets to stay?"

Farrah's eyes go deer in headlights wide as she licks her lips.

"Back up just a bit," I start. "Remember, Farrah didn't say anything about any programs being cut. She only mentioned the ones she's sure have already been approved. I'm sure she's hoping, as we all are, that the debate team will be around next year. Right Farrah?"

"Yeah, of course! We're hoping all programs get funding and it is possible that they will. The Board of Education is carefully reviewing money allocations and we are hoping to have everything in place that we have this year. Fingers crossed."

The guy on the line huffs. "So why not put all this stupid carnival money to pay for that stuff instead?"

"Like I said earlier, most of the carnival will be happening because of community donations. Businesses are donating time, services, and sponsoring parts of the carnival to make it happen. I can promise you that not one dollar of SGA or PTA money has gone toward the event. Believe me, if we could raise enough to pay for everything every student wants, we would. Be sure to check out the student portal page where many fundraising opportunities have been set up and where almost one hundred percent of money raised will go directly toward program funding."

Farrah sits back in her chair and lets out a breath.

"Thanks for your call," I say, giving her a thumbs up. "And that is great to know, Farrah. Thanks so hard for the work you and all the other members of the student government do. We are so lucky to have such strong support of the student body."

We segue into benign and safe topics, like upcoming finals and the seniors' project graduation. I wrap up with a big thanks and switch over to a short playlist as I turn off my traitorous mic and finally let my foot fall from holding the plug in position.

"Wow!" Farrah says. "That was hard. But fun too. Did I sound okay? Especially with that angry caller?"

"You did great. I think it was perfect." Minus the technical issue, which I don't mention. I swear my pulse is just now returning to normal. Why this happened today of all days, I have no idea. I hope I covered it well enough. The show must go on and all that.

"You made it feel like it was a plain old conversation, but I got this rush, being on the air. Even though I was so nervous!"

I smile, knowing exactly, of course, what she means.

"Seriously though," I say. "Thank you so much for coming on. There has been so much grumbling and worry about next year and hopefully this will help calm at least some of it for many students."

Farrah packs up and slips out of the studio just as my set of songs is ending. With my foot back on the plug and my fingers crossed, I turn on my mic, say a quick thanks to listeners and wish them a good school day ahead. My radio show is complete and my interview done. I shut everything down with a huge sigh of relief. When I step out of the room, flowers in hand, Ms.

Hudson is waiting outside. She's wearing lace leggings, a denim dress and huge hoop earrings peeking out from her hair. Not to mention a gigantic smile.

"You knocked it out of the park!" She pulls me into a hug.

"Out of the park?" I raise my eyebrows. "Did you not notice the mic cut out early in the segment?"

She smiles. "I did, but you handled it well. There was hardly any dead air before you switched over."

"And how is that going to look to WYN60?"

"Like you know how to handle a technical foul up," she says. "You could have folded and let the show end, but you recovered quickly. But enough about that, the interview was flawless. Even the way you handled the cranky caller."

"You sure?"

"Positive. You are going to knock the folks in New York dead, you know. This was your best interview yet. Very natural progression. I was working the breakfast hour in the cafeteria and I will tell you, every single person in there was listening."

Even if I wanted to, there's no way to keep the grin off my face as the energy from the morning show still pumps through me. Even the mess ups are quickly fading.

"What can I say?" I joke. "You taught me everything I know."

She squeezes my arm. "We'll chat later," she says. "Have an amazing day. You've more than earned it."

I practically skip down the hall toward my chemistry class. If a successful radio segment feels this good, I don't ever want to quit. And Ms. Hudson is right, even with the technical issues, it could have been a much worse recovery. At least I didn't freeze. I just hope that's how the folks in New York see it when they hear the lag.

I stop at my locker to drop off the flowers, smiling as I set them on the small shelf and get the books I need. I sashay toward first period, smiling at every single person I pass. I get more head nods and "good jobs," than usual, and I'm beaming as I walk down the hall, feeling more than a little like that sunshine Wes is always going on about.

My phone dings with nothing but smiley faces from Wes as I walk into chem. I slide into my seat with a huge grin and text him back, hiding the phone under the desk in case Mr. Karns comes in.

Three days of the week down and interview done! Now to wait for the inevitable horror of Saturday...

His response is nothing but another grinning smile along with a devil face. I giggle and put my phone into my bag.

14

AFTER AN AWESOME after school meeting where Ms. Hudson and I re-listen to this morning's show, I float all the way home. I cringed when I heard the few seconds of dead air when I realized the mic was out, but I'm hoping she's right and my recovery was professional enough. She confirmed that the internship has already been narrowed down to just a handful of people. So me getting this interview is beyond lucky this late in the game. The look on her face when we listened to the interview renewed my hope. If she believes I'm good enough to get this, maybe I really do have a shot.

I'm practically humming when I walk in my front door. The smell of burnt popcorn hangs in the air and other than the dripping kitchen faucet, it's quiet. Too quiet.

"Danny?" I call.

Nothing.

I step back outside. Yep. Mom's car is in the driveway. Would she have walked somewhere with him? The park down the street?

A nice thought, but fat chance.

I see her ratty brown hair draped over the arm of the couch and notice now the scratching of the needle at the end of the album again. I should throw away those few stupid albums Dad left behind. What is wrong with her? Sighing, I make my way over to her, lifting her limp arm, to expose her face: bloated, smeared eye makeup making her look like some deranged raccoon, and completely passed out. On the coffee table in front of her is all I need to know. An empty vodka bottle and a near-empty two liter of Diet Sprite. The stench of booze wafts off her. Gross.

"Great, Mom. Awesome job."

And where the hell is Danny?

I check his room, even all his favorite hiding spots, like under his bed or curled up next to his toy box.

Nothing. Panic starts to work its way through me.

Both the front and back yards are empty. I walk up and down our street quickly, peering into every yard I pass, thinking maybe he's playing outside and lost track of time. But of course, he's not. Danny is not the kind of kid to wander off and it's not like he has any neighborhood friends. My pulse drowns out all other sounds. Where the hell is he? I pick up my pace as I walk back to my house, shirt clinging with sweat.

I pull my hair up in a ponytail as I walk back inside, fanning my clammy face.

If something happened to him, I will kill her. What kind of mother—

"Incoming!" Danny's voice echoes off the tiles. He's in the bathroom!

I hear a big splash.

"Boom! Swim away! Swim away! Eeek! Shaaaaarrrrkkk at-tack!"

I burst through the bathroom door. "Danny!"

"Hey, Jazzy!" Danny squints up at me from the bathtub, plastic sharks and fish bobbing in the water around him. My breathing can't catch up to what my mind sees, but slowly, more slowly than a turtle in mud, my brain gets the telegram. Danny is okay.

But God! He may *not* have been okay. The tub, and pools, and lakes, and any other water in general, are the one and only place, the one and only unbreakable rule, we have. He cannot be in water alone. Cannot! He has to be watched carefully. If he has a seizure in water and no one is around… Well, he'll have no way to know he's under water. And he'll drown. Die. Simple as that.

Jesus, Mom.

I close the toilet lid and sit on the edge of it, watching him play with his sharks. He swims them back and forth slowly, crashing them into one another.

I take deep breaths but can't steady my brain from thinking of the what-ifs. To leave Danny in the bath like this. It's reckless. It's stupid. My fingernails dig rivets into my palms. Selfish and crazy. That's all she is.

"Jazzy, are you mad at me?"

"What?" I ask absently.

Danny stares up at me, his face as concerned as when he asks if Mommy is sick because she sleeps so much. "You have a mad face. Why are you mad? I didn't do whatever it is."

Deep breath. "You didn't do anything, buddy. How could you? It's just been a crazy day." I sit on the floor beside the tub and grab the Sponge Bob cup on the ledge. "Come here, let me wash your hair."

When I dip the cup in the water, I jump back. "Jeeez! It's freaking freezing. How long have you been in here?"

He holds out his hands. Wrinkled and purple. "I'm a raisin," he says with the lisp of missing front teeth. "So a long time? I'm doing shark races!"

"Aren't you cold? Why didn't you get out?"

Danny shrugs and tosses another shark into the air. "I was just playing, Jazzy."

I hit the drain on the tub and grab two towels from the closet. Once I pull him out and the cool air of the bathroom hits his skin, Danny starts chattering teeth and shivering. Up this close, I notice for the first time, the tinge of blue around the edge of his lips. I wrap him tightly and pick him up like a baby, joking around like I'm pretend-rocking him.

"Rock a bye Danny, on the treetop." I sing, my voice warbling with emotion at how cold he is in my arms.

"Put me down!" He laughs and laughs, that belly giggle that I love. I deposit him in his room and tell him to get dressed and meet me in the kitchen. He's still giggling when I close his door and turn my eyes upward, thanking the heavens for his resilience. And probably a good dose of plain old luck.

Scanning the mostly empty refrigerator shelves, I try to come up with a dinner plan. I'm a pretty crappy cook but I can usually pull something together. With the state my mind is in, the few things inside the fridge look like a foreign objects. I still can't wrap my mind around Danny being alone in the bathtub.

Slamming the door shut, I shoot a dirty look at Mom, passed out like a gross hobo on our couch. Then I do something I never, ever do. I open Mom's purse, then her wallet, pulling thirty dollars in fives out from her bartending tips.

I walk quickly down the hall and knock on Danny's door. "Put on socks and shoes, too. I'm taking you out."

A few minutes later, Danny and I walk out the back door, our held hands swinging between us. It may be my imagination, but even in the hot June evening, his fingers are still cold.

"STRIKE!" DANNY SCOOTS backwards, doing the little dance he does every time he bowls a spare or a strike. I high five him and match his huge grin with one of my own. I try and tamp down the sick feeling in my gut that's been swirling there since I found him alone in the tub. The bowling alley sounds are loud and distracting, balls hitting pins, music blaring. I pull apart the slices of our pizza to cool it off, putting one on my plate and one on

Danny's. My phone chimes loudly and I glare at it. If it's her, I'm not answering. Let her worry. She deserves it.

But it's Wes.

"Hey, Wes." My stomach flutters as I answer the phone. We've texted a bunch of times, but never called.

He blasts the song "Video Killed the Radio Star" into the phone.

I roll my eyes, but can't help laughing. "So dumb."

"What's up Sunny?"

It's weird, hearing his voice over the phone. I mean, it's obviously the same Wes I talk to in person, but his phone voice sounds different, slightly deeper or something.

I blow out a huge gust of air. "I'm bowling with Danny. Had to get out of my house."

"You okay? You sound weird."

I plop down on the plastic seat. "Not really. Long story. But anyway, it's my turn. I have to go."

"Where are you guys?"

"Pins and Lanes."

"Mind if I stop by?"

My stomach swirls, a tiny storm. "If you want."

"I'll be there. And call me Wes when I see you."

"As opposed to…"

"No. The way you said it, I mean. When you answered, you sounded different. I liked it." He hangs up before I can answer, and my face instantly warms. *What* way I said his name? All I did was answer the phone. I'm still shaking my head when I go up to take my turn, wondering if I've lost the touch of keeping my game face on, or in this case, my game voice. My ball rolls way right and I throw my hands up in despair.

"Gutter ball!" Danny calls happily, tomato sauce smeared on his face.

I hit two pins on my next turn and wince when I look at the score. "You're killing me. When did you get so good? Wait, come here, your shoe is untied. Let me tie it for you."

Danny puts his hands on his hips. "Really, Jazz? Like I can't tie my own shoe?"

Sure enough, he drops down and ties the laces on the hideous bowling shoes. Looking smug, he marches up to take his turn. I watch him as I nibble on my pizza, his skinny little kid self shimmying across the slippery floor. My heart swells as I think about how much Danny needs, and how unfair so much of his life is. I vow, like always, to protect every single bit of his life as much as I can. Which apparently means from Mom along with everything else he has to deal with.

We're halfway through the pizza when Wes shows up, wearing plaid shorts, a tee shirt and a Life Is Good hat, his hair curling out around the back and sides of it. He's wearing this totally honest expression too, eyes wide and a huge smile. Like, ear to ear and everything.

"Hey," he says, burying his hands in his pockets.

"Hey," I say, the stress of the afternoon unraveling so quickly, I have to sit down to keep grounded.

"Danny, you remember Wes, right? From Dr. Bee's office?"

"Yeah, and he was my roommate in the hospital!" Danny moves to slap Wes five, but Wes gives him a handshake like he'd give someone our own age.

"What's up man?" Wes says.

Danny beams at the attention before marching back up to take another turn.

Wes drops into the seat next to mine and I pass him a slice of pizza. "I don't know why we bought a whole pie. And I'm not bringing any home for my mom, either."

Wes raises his eyebrows. "Um, okay… Something happen?"

I whisper the story. My mouth stutters as much as my heart when I tell him about Mom being passed out in her drunken glory. It's not the kind of thing I really share with too many people. But the afternoon is stamped all over me, so it's not like I can hide it. And Wes obviously gets Danny's problems.

So it all pours out of me, detail after detail, coming home, her passed out, my search up and down the block for Danny. It's like slipping on the most comfortable pair of shoes to talk to someone who understands without having to explain. Wes listens intently as I reach the pinnacle of the afternoon search, eyes widening all saucer-like when I tell him about finding Danny alone in the bath. Saying it out loud makes my voice shake like we're in a 10 point on the Richter scale earthquake.

I close my eyes and take a huge, steadying breath. Nausea rises in a wave and I taste it in the back of my throat. "God, she's such an asshole. I mean, can you imagine. If... He could have..."

"He's okay," he says, putting a hand on mine. I look down at our hands without even really thinking too much about the fact that this is kind of weird, his fingers lying on top of mine like they belong there. Like it's their job to do what they're doing, giving me comfort and making me feel so much less alone. His nails are clean and neatly trimmed, his fingertips rough against my skin.

But I can't stop thinking about that stupid bath.

"Nothing happened," Wes says in this super soft voice that feels so much like a comforting hug. "Talk to her again. Remind her. I'm sure you can make her understand. I mean she must know—"

"Yeah she knows, but you don't understand, when she's like that—"

"Your turn, Jazzy!" Danny bounds over to us. I pull my hand away from Wes's quickly.

"Can Wes take my turn?" I ask my brother. "Maybe then I can come close to catching up to you."

Danny looks between us as if deciding. I pick up a paper airplane Wes left on the table and toss it at my brother. Danny catches it and throws it back with a laugh.

"I guess so," he says. "But only one turn."

"Fair enough, bro." Wes ruffles Danny's hair as he passes. Danny smiles up at him, obviously smitten with Wes's attention.

I watch the interaction with a faint smile, trying to keep my own emotions from mirroring my brother's.

15

THE WORST PART about my mom is how freaking clueless she is. Okay, that's not the worst part, since let's face it, she pretty much sucks all around. But geez. I give her the silent treatment the rest of the week and she doesn't even notice.

The night we came home from bowling she was still passed out and after putting Danny to bed I went to bed myself. What if I wasn't home? Would he have gotten out of the bath, made himself dinner? Who would have given him his medicine? I guess she just assumed I would have been home and done it all, like I always do. Or did she just not think about him or care? And God forbid he had a seizure in there. She wouldn't have even known. So I spent the next two days avoiding and ignoring her. I kept myself and Danny on track in the mornings and evenings and she worked her stupid shifts at the bar and pretty much acted like we didn't exist.

And it's not that I don't want to take care of Danny, because of course I don't mind. He's my heart. But I've been working Easy Easton Mornings all week and had afternoon meetings with Ms. Hudson to get the portfolio ready for next week's WYN60 Get Up and Go visit. So I'm stressed to the point of breaking.

When Saturday rolls around, I have no interest in getting up early. I wake up at seven to give Danny his meds and then fall back into the warm cocoon of my blankets and drift off again. I finally open my eyes again at almost lunchtime. I sit up, yawning and stretching and remembering suddenly, that today is my non-date with Wes.

I smile and look up at my ceiling.

Why I find myself poring relentlessly over my closet, I can't say for sure. Since I don't know what we're doing, I settle for a casual jean skirt and a lacy black tank top.

By early afternoon, I'm home alone and pacing the kitchen. Mom and Danny actually went somewhere together, shockingly, though I have no idea where since she seems to finally have gotten the I'm-not-talking-to-you-leave-me-alone-no-really-I-will-kill-you-with-my-deathglare memo. I don't think she even knows what she did wrong—cluelessness and aversion to actual true life details seem a natural side effect of her drinking.

But whatever. I wipe down the gold Formica and straighten the pile of papers on the counter while I look out the kitchen window for Wes's fancy SUV. I say a silent thank you prayer that Mom isn't here. I told him I didn't want him to meet her, but I'm afraid Wes's stubbornness would have made him come in to say hello. A paper on the top of the stack grabs my attention.

"Lab results?" I mutter, frowning. The date at the top is from last week. Did his labs already get here from his Dr. Bee visit? I flip through them. On the second page, one of the lines has been highlighted manually in bright yellow, by someone at the doctor's office, I guess.

"Shit."

His med levels are way up again. Damn it. This is the constant problem for Danny. He's tiny and metabolizes the medicine so quickly that he needs a ton of them to stop his seizures, but then the levels get too high, which has a whole other host of possible problems, like awful mood swings and side effects that could cause damage to his kidneys and liver. I grab a sticky note and scrawl a note for myself as much as for Mom. MUST CALL DOCTOR MONDAY ABOUT LABS!

There's not much they can do. Controlling the seizures is the most important thing, despite whatever harm to his system or organs or side effects the medicines cause. Tears burn my eyes. Why can't she handle this? Any of it? How did this huge thing become my thing?

I press down on the sticky note harder than I need to. I hate her.

A brown bag sits at the back of the counter, amid the mess of papers. I peer into it and roll my eyes. A bottle of vodka? At least she remembers some things. Like stocking up on her booze.

I fold the top of the bag back over to close it, but then I think again. I crack open the bottle and take a whiff, and the stench almost knocks me over.

Eau de Mom.

I pour almost the entire contents down the drain, leaving about 5 inches of vodka in the bottle. I pour dish detergent down the drain to try and cover the smell of liquor before filling the rest of the bottle with water. I laugh as I push the bottle to the back of the counter. She probably won't even remember she had an unopened bottle.

"Drink that," I mutter just as there's a knock at the back door.

My eyes dart around the kitchen and family room. It doesn't look great, but despite the second-hand furniture and stained carpet, it's relatively neat for the Torres house. Enough not to feel too embarrassed if he gets a glance in here from the back porch, anyway. Wes's outline is visible through Mom's gauzy door curtain, his shoulders, the flop of hair, even. I take a deep breath and the fluttering wings in my stomach settle like glitter in the bottom of a snow globe.

I open the door, standing close enough to the threshold to hopefully keep Wes from coming in and looking around.

"Hey!" I say. A little too enthusiastically.

"Hey." His hands are buried in his pockets and he's wearing that half smirk, half smile that is really starting to get to me, like stirring way deep in my belly get to me. It stays on his face for a second longer and I squirm, hoping the way my insides are flopping around isn't obvious. He takes a step back.

"Whoa," he says. "That's some outfit."

My face instantly goes all pie-just-out-of-the-oven hot. He's wearing jeans and a white tee shirt and I'm hoping I'm not dressed wrong for whatever we're doing. I gesture to my skirt. "Is this okay? I wasn't sure what we were doing. I can change."

"Oh, don't worry. I have some awful stuffed planned for us." He grins. "You will have the worst time of your life. But no, please don't change. It may not be the best choice for our plans, but my conscience will not allow me to let you change into anything other than that skirt."

Helllllo, listeners. Welcome to—wait, what did he say?

"Don't look at me like that," he says with a shrug. "I'm human. And a guy. I appreciate what I see is all. I'm allowed that, no?"

"No," I answer as I lock the door. "Checking out your friend is weird."

Not that I didn't notice the way his tee shirt fits just right across his chest and back.

"Let's go," I say.

Smirk smile. Smile smirk.

Jesus. He's cute.

This is not a good start to this supposed non-date. I shake my head as I push past him toward the car.

Wes's eyes have a mischievous twinkle as he moves toward the passenger door. I elbow him, but I'm smiling now and laughter sits on the edge of my lips. "I can open my own door."

I settle into the luxurious leather and pull the visor down to check my lip gloss. Wes crosses behind the car and I watch him in the mirror. I try to ignore the smallest of smiles still dancing on my lips in my reflection.

"Where to?" I say as the engine roars to life.

"Just you wait." Wes pulls away from the curb.

We drive for twenty minutes, turning off one highway and onto another and then changing onto yet another again. We head so far east, the New York skyline looms larger with each passing mile, but he gets off before that, turning onto side streets in a strange looking, industrial-type town I've never seen. My curiosity is practically strangling me, but there's no way I'm giving him the satisfaction of asking. I pick at a loose thread on the hem of my skirt instead.

Wes changes the radio station endlessly, going between pop, hip hop, country, and oldies stations. He shakes his head, frowning. "Never anything good on."

"I am so making a playlist for next time."

Wes turns toward me, his eyes bright and meeting mine before flicking back to the road. "Next time?"

I huff and wave a hand. "Oh you know what I mean."

Damn it. He knew exactly what I meant. Even if I didn't.

We turn down a deserted street, nothing but a few factories that look like they've been closed since before my mom was born. The buildings eventually give way to large fenced areas that go on for what looks like miles. He shifts into park with way more drama than necessary and wearing a hey-I-think-I'm-so-cool grin. I crane my neck to look to the top of the fence. It's at least 15 feet high with barbed wire on the top.

What the what?

"Um, wow. You really shouldn't have…"

"Come on." He climbs out of the car and waits for me by the chain link.

"What is this? A garbage dump?" I ask.

"Close!" Wes waves behind him as if he is giving a tour. "I'd like to welcome DJ Sunny Torres to the Garden State's largest junkyard."

"Largest junkyard." I deadpan.

"Is there anything less date-like than junk?"

I cross my arms and squint through the fence. "Oh my God," I say. "We are literally hanging out and looking at garbage." I drop my head in my hands. My laugh vibrates against my palms.

Wes taps my toe with his shoe. "Come on."

When I look up at him, he's all expectant like a cat that's delivered a dead rabbit and is waiting for a scratch behind the ears.

Still laughing, I shake my head. "Okay, I guess?"

I follow him down the crumbling sidewalk, kicking dusty gravel along the way. We reach the junkyard's gate and Wes gently pushes one side open, the lock and chain hanging.

"This isn't illegal, is it?"

Wes gently touches the small of my back as the gate falls closed behind us. "Not exactly. I have friends who know people. So we get to take our own private tour."

I can't help but laugh. "You really are a dork," I say.

We walk around a particularly huge pile of old appliances in various states of disrepair. I stare, kind of amazed at the pile of old refrigerators and dishwashers.

"This is pretty much the weirdest place I've ever been."

"Ooh, look!" Wes darts down the next aisle. I hurry to catch up to where he stands, staring at what looks like a pile of metal. Across the way, what appears to be rusty car parts sit in piles and I even see shells of actual, whole cars at the end of the row.

"I don't get it?"

Wes kicks a large scrap of metal. "It's an old propeller." He squats down and runs his hand along the side of it. "Definitely an old prop plane. Probably a turbo prop." He squints up at the pile behind the propeller, eyes darting back and forth along the scraps.

"See anything you like?" I snort.

He looks at me with animated eyes. "Come on, this is cool! You don't think it's cool? There's probably all kinds of plane parts here."

"Very cool," I agree, humoring him.

"Anyway," he says, dusting his hands off and standing up. "We have other places to go."

"You mean there's more than this?"

"Very funny. Yes, there's more. So was this a bad enough time for you?"

"It was cool," I say as we walk back to the gate. "But I figure it can only go up from here."

He beeps the car alarm to unlock the doors and gives me a wry smile. "You say that now," he says. "But you don't know where we're going next."

I'M NOT SURE what could possibly top the garbage trip, but Wes chuckles as he drives to our next destination. When he pulls into Heaven's Doorway Cemetery (Where All Your Dreams Live On), I actually feel my eyes widen and my mouth drop open.

"Um, Wes. I'm all for the jokes, but I don't think I can hang out in a graveyard, even if it is the middle of the afternoon."

"Come on, Sunny. Live a little." he grins, waiting. "See what I did there... *Live* a little?"

I groan.

"Trust me." He pulls the car to the side of the driveway between the gravestone section and the mausoleum section. "I know it's creepy, but I have a plan."

"A plan? Seems you really took my not if you were the last living guy on earth thing pretty seriously, huh?" I joke.

"Desperate times," he answers as he pulls a large tote and his backpack from the car.

I follow him to a clearing under a big tree. He pulls a blanket from the tote and I help him unfold it. I'm happy this spot at least seems reserved for visitors, instead of us actually sitting on top of someone's grave. But still, being the only two living people around thousands of dead? It's freaky.

I sit square in the middle of the blanket with my back to the mausoleums. All around me, graves and statues make up the landscape as far as I can see. I focus on Wes instead, as he pulls item after item from his backpack.

"What is all this?" I pick up a container and peer through the plastic. It's filled with various cheeses

"Snacks," he says as he lays items out on the blanket. "I followed your rules. No meals, you said. So we'll have snacks. Here, help me open these up."

I open the cheese and a box of crackers while Wes lays out grapes and popcorn and even pita chips with guacamole.

"Wow. You really thought of everything."

Wes's smile stretches wide. "And there's drinks, too." He drags the tote closer to the blanket, and pulls out a small cooler, opening it to reveal a bunch of choices: water, iced tea, soda, juice. "I wasn't sure what you liked." He takes off his Life Is Good hat and scratches the back of his head, making his messy hair even more chaotic.

What I like? Many things I probably shouldn't. Like him. The thought pokes from the recesses of my mind, from some corner where I've apparently tried to hide it. And it's true, even if I only admit it to myself and even if my heart is terrified of liking another boy after Sebastian. I can't help it. I like Wesley McEnroe. Definitely more than I should.

But I simply pull a bottle of water from the cooler and smile.

After we've stuffed ourselves with snacks, Wes folds a paper towel into a floppy airplane. He tosses it at me, but it flops onto the blanket without taking flight. He shrugs and lies down on the blanket, dropping his hat over his eyes.

"So, Sunny Torres. Tell me something about you I don't know."

"Like what?" I ask. "What you see is what you get, really."

He tips his hat back and opens one eye to look at me. "Why do I not believe that?"

I toss his paper towel airplane at him, hitting him square in the stomach. Leaning back on my elbows, I cross my legs at the ankles. "My life is a chaotic mess? Not that that's a big secret."

"Did you ever talk to your mom about the other night?"

"Nope. And you know what? I don't even think she knows what she did. She is clueless. I did pour out almost a whole bottle of her vodka though. And filled it back up with water."

Wes rolls onto his side, his eyes squinting with laughter. "You didn't!"

"Hell yeah I did." I polish my nails on my shirt. "Let this be a warning. Don't mess with me."

"Noted."

"Whatever with her, anyway. This week is going to be crazy busy with radio stuff. Plus, next week, I have my city trip for the Get up and Go interview. I don't even have time to worry about my stupid mother. As long as I can keep Danny safe, that's all I care about."

Wes drops his hat over his face again. "Yeah, I get that. But it shouldn't have to be like that. You know?"

"Yeah, well…"

"Seriously, I'm sure if—"

"Can you not? Please? My home life, my mom… it's all beyond repair right now. It's not like I haven't tried."

"But—"

"Please, Wes. Don't ruin this by talking about her. She doesn't get to intrude on this."

He tips his hat back and gives me another of my favorite grins. I breathe deeply, hoping this means the family topic is dropped.

"Fair enough," he says. He flips the hat in the air and catches it. "So this internship is a really huge thing, huh?"

"Um, yeah! It's the Get Up and Go show, right? On WYN60? It's a summer internship working there at the station doing whatever interns do. But, not only would it be a dream come true for me to spend my summer there, my teacher said it would look really good for my college stuff, especially since I need to get a scholarship if I have any hope of going to school. I don't want to go anywhere super expensive or anything. Hopefully a commuter state school, so I can live at home and be close to Danny. All I need is a good communications program and a radio station, but even still, I need this experience."

"I'm sure you'll get it," Wes says, propped up on one elbow. "You're awesome on the radio."

"Yeah, probably me and everyone else going for it."

"Is there a lot of competition?"

"From what I hear, there were hundreds of applicants, maybe thousands, but it's already been narrowed down to a handful. None from my school applied, thankfully. Our radio program is pretty small and other than me, no one is too serious about it at our school. That's why I get so much airtime as a junior. But there are some schools around here with some kick ass station presence, like Chester High and the infamous Big D, who is a serious pain in my ass at beating me out on stuff. God I hope she's not a finalist. Not to mention any high school DJs in the city. Let's face it, my chances are probably pretty slim."

"I still think you're better than you realize. At least you know what you want to do. Your mom must be happy about that."

I snort. "*My* mom? You're kidding, right?"

"Sorry. I didn't mean it like that. It's just, my mom is always pressuring me about colleges. It's driving me crazy. She has college tour after tour lined up, some crazy good schools too, that are really hard to get into."

"Yeah but you're in AP classes, I bet you have perfect grades."

"Nearly perfect. Like me."

"Dork." I toss another of his paper towel airplanes at his face and miss.

"Seriously, school has always been really easy for me. But that doesn't mean I like it."

"So why don't you tell her? Your mom seems cool."

"She's cool, but the pressure is crazy. I'm an only child and she likes everything to be perfect. Including my future. She has it all mapped out in her mind. My choice of colleges, my major, even a list of places where I'll possibly work after I graduate."

Wow. That's intense.

"But what do *you* want?"

He shrugs. "I have no idea. But I don't want to know yet, you know? I want to, like, take a year off or something, before I figure it out. I'm seriously sick of school and the idea of working in an office for the rest of my life sounds like pure torture. What's the point of college unless I'm willing to sell my soul to do something I hate? I just want some time to figure it out, before I go."

Wes's phone starts playing some really loud, really angry heavy metal music.

"What is that?" A giggle bursts out of me as he pulls the phone from his pocket and the music gets louder, but I'm full on laughing when he stands up and starts dancing and head banging and air guitar movements. He hops up on the bench and mimes crowd diving, hands out as if he's going to fall right on top of our picnic.

I laugh harder, arms wrapped around my stomach, which is starting to ache from flexing my out-of-practice laughing muscles.

"Just a reminder I set. Be right back." Wes holds up a finger as he continues to thrash and dance toward the car. The music fades as he crosses the lane and opens the passenger door.

I hiccup one last laugh, but every time I picture him, with long hair smashing a guitar or something, I start laughing again.

I stare out at the headstones all around us, remembering suddenly, exactly where we are. I'm not sure what it says about Wes or myself, but it's like I'd forgotten we were sitting in the middle of a cemetery all this time. I toss his hat between my hands, my favorite bangles jingling on my wrist. Propping the hat on my head, I breathe in the scent of him and kind of like the way his familiar accessory feels on me.

After a few minutes, he's still in his car. He's sitting in the passenger seat, looking down, his face very serious. Or... wait.

Is he okay? I squint, trying to make sure he actually is looking down and not passed out... or something worse.

Worry twists the pit of my stomach and I jump up from the blanket to get a better look across the road. He's not moving. My nails dig into my palms, my shoulders aching with tension.

Please no. Please.

I'm halfway to the car when Wes looks up at me with a broad smile that stops me right in the middle of the road. But it's relief that makes my heart and breathing stutter all over each other like they're in a three-legged race.

He's okay, Jasmine. He's as safe and healthy as he ever is.

But even with the proof right in front of me, my mind won't slow down enough for me to fully believe it. Or be okay with the possibility of what could have happened. Wes is healthy, he hasn't had a seizure in years. But have I relied too much on that fact? Could the very real possibility of having someone else in my life with seizures be too much for me to handle? I can barely handle the weight of worry strapped to me because of Danny. What if I did get closer to Wes and something terrible happened to him? I can't handle worrying this much about someone else.

God, I'm a horrible person. A horrible, insensitive person.

"Miss me?" He slides out of the car and closes the door, moving to the trunk to drop something into a small duffle bag.

I raise a brow, still trying to calm myself down. I have to play it cool though. The last thing I need is him seeing through me to what I was thinking. So I laugh instead. "What are you up to over here? Was the heavy metal alarm something I should be concerned about?"

Wes zips the duffel and slams the back door. He tilts his head. "If I didn't know better, I'd say you were suspicious of me, Ms. Torres."

I roll my eyes and turn back toward our picnic. "Oh fine," I say. "Keep your secrets, then."

My heart is still stuttering, and not just with worry. Unease ripples through me as I think about his words. After what Sebastian pulled, I do have some trust issues. I hate that he's done that to me, made me wary and untrusting. But I don't think I have to feel that way with Wes. And that scares me.

A lot of things about Wes scare me.

I kneel on the blanket and start to gather all our garbage into one of the plastic shopping bags.

"It was my meds," Wes says quietly. "The song was the dumb alarm to remind me. It's a safety net alarm since I almost never forget to take them. But I should have had them at four o'clock, and I didn't, so this is always set to remind me, just in case. What can I say, DJ Sunny. You distracted me to the point of self harm." He grins his wide grin, but it doesn't reach his eyes this time. He shifts on the blanket, his body only inches from mine. I can feel the heat of him when I lean forward to clear away more crumbs.

I look down at my hands as they wipe the blanket. Wes stills my hand with one of his, threading our fingers together. "Hey, don't look so scared, Sunny. I'm fine."

"I know," I whisper, looking at the way our fingers twine together. He seems so strong, so healthy. But the fact that he *could* have a seizure is just below the surface of all that. I take a shaky breath. I don't want it to matter, but I can't help it, it does.

"I'm a worrier, what can I say?"

"Seriously, stop worrying so much. Don't be a middle-aged teenager."

I pull my hand from his and sit up, hands on hips. "Middle aged? If that's your idea of a pickup line, you really need some help."

"Pickup line, huh? What do I need one of those for?"

"Oh shut up," I wave him away, my cheeks burning. "You know what I mean!" I turn to my bag and look through it for some imaginary item to keep me from making eye contact. When I finally look up, he's chewing a pretzel rod and grinning.

"Shut up," I say again.

He moves his eyebrows up and down and plucks the pretzel from his mouth, pretending to knock ashes off it, cigar-style.

My smile spreads slowly, like a flower opening, my cheeks aching with how wide it is.

"So, we should probably go before it gets dark and too creepy for even me," Wes says. "But, I have to ask, was it a bad enough time for you? I mean, I wanted it to be as non-date awful as possible."

"The truth?" I say. I decide, right then, to be honest, real.

Wes chews on his thumbnail and pretends to contemplate the question. "Nah, lie to me."

I roll my eyes. "Graveyard or not, this is kind of perfect. Even without the heavy metal dancing, which, not gonna lie, was one of the best parts."

He throws up a rock and roll sign and bobs his head as if he's going to break out in dance again.

"Yeah," I say. "Even without that. This weirdo, non-date, cemetery picnic is probably the nicest thing anyone has done for me in a really long time."

Wes's smile is like the pulse of airwaves broadcasting to a really huge audience. I mean, you can feel the strength of it, like a zillion decibels.

He picks up the cooler and I drape the folded blanket over my arm. We walk to the car, only a few inches of space between us.

"Glad it was a good time," he says.

"Best non-date ever," I agree.

"Nice hat, by the way." He knocks his shoulder into mine. My face goes hot as I bring my hand to my head. I had completely forgotten I was wearing it.

"Keep it on," he says. "You look cute in it."

But I pull it off when we reach the car and shake my hair out. I give his messy, every-which-way hair an exaggerated scowl. "You need it more than I do," I say, plopping his hat back onto his head.

Smile smirk. Smile smirk.

Sigh.

It's not until we're back on the highway and headed toward home that my stomach starts churning with the reality of Mom and everything else I have to get back to. Wes's hand inches toward mine during the drive, but never quite reaches. I'm not sure if I'm happy about that or not.

16

MONDAY MORNING I'M back on the radio with a new idea for a fun segment I can carry over the next few days. Thankfully Mr. Tony replaced the offending wall plug, so hopefully I'll have no more microphone malfunctions.

"Good morning, Easton High! It's Jasmine Torres with your Easy Easton Mornings show. In the last week we've discussed friendships, and school politics and even broken hearts. Today I'd like to turn the tables and talk about the best of things. Love is often in the halls here at Easton, despite the school's strict rules on PDA. Ha ha ha. Anyone out there have a secret crush? I am declaring this week love week on the morning show, with today dedicated solely to secret crushes. Have a dedication for the secret of your admiration? Write to Eastonmornings at Easton dot edu and tell me your story and dedication. We will get it on the airwaves and get your crush closer to knowing where they stand."

I hit play on the short playlist of love songs I've cued up and turn to my computer, hoping I get some good dedications. I mean, it's high school. There have got to be some secret admirers around here. Let's hope they fess up and give me something good to work with.

I yawn and take a big gulp of my coffee. Last night I got basically no sleep. Mom was working, thankfully, because I'm still not speaking to her, and anyway things feel so much calmer and better when she isn't around. Danny and I played Wii dance for about two hours before he finally went to sleep. After that I caught up on homework and then ended up chatting online with Wes until way past my normal sleep time.

My phone buzzes on the desk.

"Speak of the devil." I smile at the screen, excitement zinging through my belly.

can I make a dedication?

My finger hovers over the screen. The phone dings again.

i know you're reading this. do i make u too nervous to respond? ;)

I huff a big breath, fingers flying over the keys.

smartass. i'm busy.
rigggggghhhhht.
gotta go! dedication line open for easton students only.

I turn the phone face down so I'm not distracted as I turn back to the microphone.

"Our first batch of dedications are coming in. Here is one dedicated to 'the red-haired beauty in my algebra class,' from 'looks dorky but is really sweet.'" I hit play on the song and sit back, grabbing my phone with a smile.

fine. no dedication. but i can't stop thinking about what you said last night.
what i said? what?
all of it. i can't stop thinking about YOU.

My breath catches.

yeah?

What else can I say? God I'm so bad at this. The phone dings again and I read quickly, my smile spreading through me like the warmest syrup.

let me take you out. for real.

I start to type no. But I backspace and delete it. Can it really hurt? We've already hung out, and it's not like our non-dates were really non-dates, right? Wes is so much fun. And I really do like him. Scared or not.

Wes texts again before I can respond:

trust me.

It's simple and I want to. I really really want to.

this time I'll make it a good date.

Take a breath. Fingers hover. To be honest? Or to joke around?

okay. but p.s. the last one was good too.

I put the phone down, knowing I admitted way more than I meant to with my response. But as I scroll through the dedications in the morning show's inbox, I can't help wondering if it was a mistake.

When I get home from school, Mom isn't there yet. I throw in a load of Danny's laundry since he was whining about being out of tee shirts this morning.

"Aannnd, we have no detergent left." I slam the washer shut and go in search of my purse. I have less than four bucks in my wallet, which isn't going to get me far. I drop onto the stool in the kitchen. Damn it, Mom.

I finish my homework just as Danny walks in the back door. Like always, he heads to his room for an after school nap after taking his medicine. Even though I should be voted most likely to stay busy, I decide that a nap is exactly what I need too. I head to my room and fall asleep almost the instant I pull my comforter over myself.

Is there anything worse than being woken up by screaming?

For one terrified minute I jump up, thinking something is wrong with Danny. But then I realize my mom is in the kitchen, going ballistic. I hear my name more than once.

I stumble into the kitchen rubbing my eyes. Danny sits at the table, pencil frozen over a math worksheet while he stares at Mom, pacing by the sink.

"There you are!" she says, her eyes as wild as her hair.

I drop into the seat next to Danny's and look at his homework. She still doesn't deserve me talking to her.

"Jasmine Luz," she says. "I am talking to you."

Oooh, middle name. Did you hear that, listeners? Looks like someone showed up on the let's pretend to be a mom show today!

"Great job," I say to Danny. "Looks like they're all right so far."

"Subtraction is hard," he says with a frown.

"Jasmine!"

Danny jumps in his chair, and for that I am angry. I turn in my seat. "What do you want?"

She holds the vodka bottle in front of her. "Do you know what happened to this?"

"To what?" I ask innocently. I have to admit I'm surprised she figured it out. But, I'm happy, too. She deserves to be upset.

"Very funny young lady." She puts the bottle down and wags a finger at me. "If you remember, I am the one who works and pays the bills around here."

I snort. "Yeah. You do so much."

"What's with your attitude lately? I am still your mother you know!"

Hardly.

"Hey, Danny. Can you go take a shower before dinner? I'll help you finish these problems after?"

He looks up at me with a questioning expression. I never ask him to shower before dinner.

"Go on," I say sternly. "I'll make you mac and cheese?"

With the promise of his favorite meal, he is out the door faster than you can say processed, bright orange, cheese-flavored powder.

"What the hell was that about?" Mom's nostrils flare.

I hold up a finger. "Wait," I say, venom dripping from the word.

When I hear the shower start and hear Danny start singing his favorite Disney songs I step closer to Mom.

"You," I say. "Need to get your drinking under control. It's out of hand. I am sick of being the sister *and* the mom around here."

She steps back as if I've slapped her, but anger darkens her expression. "Excuse me? How dare you!"

"Danny could have died!" I scream.

"What are you talking about?"

"Are you that freaking clueless? Last week. I came home and he was in the bathtub, mom. The bathtub! The water was ice cold and he had been playing in there a long time. You were passed out in your drunken glory, slobber and vodka all over the couch with the stupid record player turning. If he had a seizure in there! God. I can't even say it." I press the heels of my hands against my eyes as the sobs rock through me. When I finally look back up at her, she stares out the window.

"You have no right to say these things to me," she says. "And no idea what it's like to be a single mother to you and your brother."

"Are you kidding?"

She turns on her heel and stares at me. "Excuse me?"

"For your information," I say, practically snarling. "I know *exactly* what it feels like to be a single mother."

She glares at me, arms crossed. "What is that supposed to mean?"

"Who do you think is doing all the mom things around here! The homework, the doctors, the cooking, the laundry. You can't even stay sober long enough to make sure your son doesn't die in the bathtub! And God forbid I have to leave and get to school early like a normal freaking kid. You don't even wake up to see if he eats breakfast and in the meantime he's having a seizure for who knows how long. Jesus, Mom. If it wasn't for me, who knows what would have happened to him by now!"

"Jasmine!"

"No, Mom! You need to wake up. It started when Dad left, but guess what? He's not coming back! Get over it. Stop playing those stupid three albums he left behind. Sell the stupid stereo so we can pay for some things. He doesn't want you! He doesn't want us! Grow up and start being a mother! You have a family here that wants you, that needs you! Right here! Us! What would have happened to Danny, Mom, if I wasn't here that day? And all the others! What? Tell me! What would have happened to him by now!"

"Jasmine. Stop it. Stop this!" Tears stream down her cheeks and her eyes are wild and frantic, like a trapped animal.

"No! I'm not going to stop." I'm screaming now. I feel like a crazy girl. Bona fide psychotic. "Act like a mother! Stop making me do everything! Why can't you just be freaking normal so I can have a regular life!"

"Jazzy?"

My head whips around to Danny, standing in the doorway, a towel draped around his little body while he drips shower water onto the floor.

"Why are you so mad? I heard you yelling from the shower." Danny's eyes are wide with terror and filled with tears. "Don't be mad, Jazzy. I'm sorry you have to help with my homework and cook and stuff. I can try to do those things on my own. Don't cry."

My heart feels very wrong, like it's doing something really dangerous, like losing its ability to beat. I drop to my knees in front of him and take his small hands in mine.

"No! Danny. That's not what I meant. We were having a grown up conversation. That's not what we were saying at all."

His little bottom lips quivers, brown eyes wide and framed by still-wet lashes. "I don't want to make you mad, Jazzy. I love you. You don't have to do all that stuff for me." He throws his arms around me and I pull him into a tight hug.

"No way, kid. I *love* spending time with you and helping you with stuff. It's hands down always the best part of my day."

Danny pulls back and looks at me skeptically but a small smile pulls the corners of his mouth up.

"Okay?" I ask, trying to keep the tremor from my voice. I can't believe all the stuff he probably heard me say. My legs shake as if they'll give out and dump me on the floor to do what I really feel like doing, crumpling into a ball to cry. But I take a deep breath and steady myself. Forget radio. I should be an actress. "I have to go out for a little bit. Do you mind if Mom does the homework with you tonight?"

Danny looks up at me and then to Mom. His gaze volleys between us for a minute. Mom, I will admit, smiles reassuringly and puts out a hand.

"Go get dressed," she says, unable to control the shaking in her own voice. "Mac and cheese, right? And math homework?"

Danny smiles tentatively and looks at me again as if he's scared. Probably plain old confused. It's not like she's ever around for the normal day-to-day stuff like homework.

"It'll be okay," I say. "You'll have a good night and I'll be home soon."

"Okay." He looks down at the ground. His disappointment is like an arrow to my heart, but I can't stay here. I'll explode if I do.

Hands on his shoulders, I turn him toward his room and kiss the top of his head. "You still have a little shampoo in your hair, Danny. You smell good, but you might want to rinse it."

As soon as I hear Danny in his room I turn back to Mom. "I'll be back," I say.

"You aren't taking my car." The cool edge to her voice is like a knife. "I may screw up a lot, but no one is perfect. And I am your mother and will not let you talk to me that way."

I stare into her eyes. I could point out the obvious: the fact that her own son isn't comfortable having her cook dinner and do homework with him. Or the fact that I'm truly the only reliable one here. But I think she knows these things and after the look on Danny's face and the fact that I put it there, I don't want to keep this argument going. I need to get out of here. Because she may not be perfect, but I obviously hugely screwed up tonight too.

"I'll walk." I grab my phone from the counter.

"You have a curfew." A tremor shakes her voice again.

It takes everything in me not to roll my eyes. I may have crossed the line, but I'm right here, and we both know it. Without me, this whole family, what's left of us, would have fallen apart. And that's being generous.

"Yep. See you later." I close the door behind me.

I walk through my entire neighborhood more than once, around and around and back again, making sure to stay far away from Sebastian's block. After half an hour I have nowhere else to go, but I still don't want to go home. I stop at the corner playground and sit on the swings I've been sitting on my whole life. I swipe my cell phone on and call Frankie. No answer. She's probably at the church with her mom. I text her.

You around?

Nothing.

I twist the swing into a tight coil and let it unwind, spinning me around and around. I can't get Danny's hurt expression out of my mind. What is wrong with me? How could I have let her get me that mad? Even if he was in the shower, I should have known there was a chance he could hear us.

Stupid, stupid, stupid.

I hope he believed me before I left. The idea of hurting him, in any way, is enough to bring my tears to the surface again. I wipe them away and try to come up with a plan. What can I do to get through to her? To make things normal? Is she that selfish that we don't matter to her at all? I don't think I should have to accept that this is the way things are going to be. It's not fair.

Round and round my thoughts go. But they lead me nowhere.

I scroll through my contacts again. When I see Wes's name, I hit call.

HIS CAR PULLS up a few minutes later. He walks toward me, pushing his dirty blond hair back. In his other hand, he has a bulky paper bag. Curiosity lifts my mood and I give him a small smile.

"Sorry to bother you." I twist again on the swing.

"What? You're crazy. You're no bother." He puts the bag on the ground and sits on the swing next to mine. "You okay?"

I shrug. I picture Danny's sad and scared face again and a sob lodges in my chest.

"She's so clueless, you know?"

"Your mom?"

"Yeah. She screws up and it's not cool. It's serious. And I love my brother and I do everything I can. But I can't always be there. I mean, I try. But one day I won't be there when it matters and when she isn't bothering or passed out or something and then what?"

Beside me, Wes's silent.

"But tonight I screwed up. I was fighting with her and I thought Danny was in the shower but he wasn't anymore and he heard me. If you could have seen his expression..." I drop my face into my hands, shaking it back and forth against my palms. "Man, I suck."

"Hey, stop. You so don't suck. You're a great sister. You're taking care of him, which means so much. It's a lot more than most teenage sisters would do."

"It's not fair," I whisper.

I can't believe I even said that out loud. I love Danny so much and I want to keep him safe and healthy. But the fact that it's all on me isn't fair.

Wes nods. "You're right. It's not fair. You deserve to just be you, totally beautiful, seventeen-year-old, you."

He blurs in my vision and I quickly swipe at my tears.

Beautiful? I raise my eyes to his.

"Come on, don't look at me like that. You know you're beautiful."

I shake my head. "You're crazy," I whisper.

But he's more things, too. Like sweet, and kind. And here when I need him.

"I get how you feel," he says. "My life hasn't exactly been all fun times either. It sucks to have the childhood and fun stolen away with doctors and tests and stupid, strict, keep-Wes-safe-in-case-of-a-seizure rules. We should be doing stupid stuff, like drinking beer and jumping off rooftops."

"Jumping? Off rooftops?"

"Okay, maybe that's taking it too far." He laughs, reaching down for the bag at his feet. "But you know what I mean. You shouldn't have to be weighed down by your family, just like I shouldn't have to listen to my mom go on and on about college applications or about my epilepsy all the time. That weighs me down, too. Big time."

Guilt stabs at me over letting his epilepsy worry me the way it did the other night. The way it does.

"Yeah," I say. "Should could would, whatever that expression is. Our lives are what they are, right?"

"Maybe. Maybe not."

I look over at him. His eyes glint with moonlight and excitement.

"Let's make a pact. From here on out, no worries?"

"Seriously, Wes. *Me?* Not worry?"

He sighs, swinging the paper bag in his hands. "Fine, worry is allowed, but when you're with me, can you at least try to forget about it? Can we try and act like we have normal lives, and had normal childhoods and even normal families?"

He gets it. I nod, his face going blurry in my vision again. Maybe he's right. Maybe I can push some of the worries away.

"And hopefully your mom will get her crap together soon."

"Yeah, in your house where things are normal, that may seem possible, but try a day in the life with the Torres family and you'll be singing a different tune." I sniff back tears.

"I don't think you want me to sing," Wes says. "You've seen my dancing and I assure you, my singing is leagues worse."

A vision of his head banging dance flashes through my mind and I smile. He opens the bag as I wipe the tears from my cheeks.

"So anyway," he says. "I stopped at Clyde's."

Despite being upset and still trying to forget the last few hours, I perk up.

"How did you know I like Clyde's?"

Wes shakes his head. "Lucky guess? Who, in a twenty mile radius of Clyde's doesn't know and love it? Homemade ice cream in over a hundred flavors? What's not to love?"

When he pulls out four sundae cups, my mouth literally waters.

"But," he says. "Guessing what flavor you'd like was not easy."

"Why did you get so many?" I laugh. "Are more people coming I don't know about?"

Wes holds up a finger giving me a faux exasperated look. "Would you listen?"

I nod, both hands over my mouth as if to hold any more interruptions or laughter in.

"First," he says. "I got apple pie ice cream sundae. Vanilla ice cream with pieces of pie crust and baked apples inside. It's one of their most popular choices. But, it's also traditional, so I wasn't sure it quite suited you, since you're so obviously *not* traditional."

"But—"

He holds up a hand to stop me and I clamp my mouth shut again.

"Next up, brownie batter with peanut butter. Regular chocolate seemed too boring for you, but hey, brownie batter, just because. Who doesn't like to eat batter? Batter-flavored anything sounded good to me. Third, we have raspberry chocolate chip. Their raspberry is kind of super sour and also super sweet, so then I thought you can sometimes be that way too…"

"Very funny!" I'm laughing harder now, but something else is happening inside me too. My walls are crumbling, bit by bit, as if they are nothing more than walls of straw instead of stone and brick. I'm reminded of the old children's fable, except Wes isn't the big bad wolf at all.

Not every boy will be like Sebastian.

One by one, Wes lines the sundae cups along on the railroad ties that separate the swing sets from the rest of the playground.

"Now, our last choice is the one that I actually picked first. For some reason, this one says DJ Sunny Torres to me. Let's see how well I know you, shall we?" He pulls the last cup out and waves it in front of me. "Mango ice cream. It's not only delicious, but it's also kind of sassy, and sunny, too."

My mouth is full on watering now and when I hop off the swing to reach for the cup, I'm a little too excited and almost knock the glorious mango ice cream right out of his hands.

"It's my favorite," I admit, taking the cup and spoon from him.

"That would explain the reaction." He pumps his fist. "I knew it! Am I good or what?"

When I take a bite of the ice cream, I close my eyes. "So good."

Wes opens the brownie batter cup and we sit back on the swings. "Wow, that is damn good," he says through a mouth full of ice cream.

"Better than good," I say. "But Wes?"

"Yeah?"

151

"Who's going to eat the rest of those?"

"Um... us?" He looks up at the sky, avoiding my eyes in a pretend serious and guilty way.

"Also, did you just refer to this ice cream as sassy?"

Swinging slightly in my direction, he hangs his head and I fixate on the bit of brownie batter ice cream on the corner of his lip. I think about what it would be like to lick it off.

Hellllo, listeners! What in the world is going on in Jasmine Torres' mind tonight?

"I did, didn't I?" Wes grins. "Don't tell anyone I used the word sassy. Damn, you bring out the best—or is it the worst—in me, Sunny."

I shake my head as I continue to eat my ice cream.

Once it's all gone, and by all I mean all four cups, Wes climbs to the top of the curly slide like he's a little kid. I lounge in the grass near the bottom, unable to move after all that ice cream and still feeling rattled by the scene at home. Checking the time on my phone, I hope Danny got his homework done and ate dinner okay. And that his heart isn't broken by the things he heard me say.

"I'm the king of the universe!" Wes shouts from the top of the slide. I smile as much as possible while thinking of Danny's sad face.

Suddenly Wes's heavy metal music fills the park. Still on the top of the slide's platform, he holds his phone out like a speaker and does his dorky, hilarious oh-my-God-why-is-he-dancing-like-that thing and my laughter comes back, full force like a hurricane wind that will knock me over. I lean back on the grass, my laughter coming in fits as Wes continues to entertain me. I sit up when the music stops. Wes slides down the slide, landing right in front of me. I'm still giggling when he pulls me up to stand. He holds onto my hands tightly, hooking his fingers with mine.

"Those are some serious dance moves." My words are barely more than a breath. Wes's eyes lock on mine before he lowers his gaze to my lips. He lets go of one of my hands and reaches up to tuck my hair behind my ears.

"You feel better?" He asks softly, taking another step, even closer.

"I do. I really do. It was so nice of you to come here. To do all this." I gesture to the empty ice cream cups.

He pulls me closer and I let myself be pulled. I lean against him and wrap my arms around his waist in a tight hug, my ear taking in the thump thump thump of his heartbeat. His hands, warm and strong, massage my shoulders and his arms circle me tightly. He rests his chin on the top of my head and I take a deep, deep breath, breathing in his laundry detergent and the scent of him, boy out of shower, some kind of musky soap. And comfort. Just straight up comfort. This feels way too good. Way too safe.

"Thanks," I whisper against him, blinking rapidly against his soft tee shirt to stop the tears that threaten to come for an entirely different reason this time.

17

I WAKE UP the next morning and swear my house is on fire, based on smell alone. Once I'm actually awake and standing in the middle of my room, I realize all is safe and well when I figure out what the smell is—someone is cooking bacon.

What the—? Still half asleep, I stumble into the kitchen. Mom stands at the stove, spatula in hand.

Good morning, listeners. Join me, DJ Jasmine Torres as I broadcast on location, from the Twilight Zone!

Seriously though. This is weird. It's the first time I've seen her since last night's argument and I'm not sure what to say.

"Hi. Mom." Safe.

She turns around with a smile on her face. "Hey Jazz. You hungry? I'm making pancakes. And bacon."

I nod slowly. Who are you and what have you done with my real mother? "Yeah. Wow. Sounds good. I'll get ready and be back in a few."

My phone dings on my desk. Frankie confirming our after school plans. I'm going to her house to borrow a good interview outfit. The one I had planned for the field trip is nowhere near good enough for a one-on-one actual interview meeting.

My phone dings again and I pick it up, ready to tell her I have to get ready. But it's Wes. I grin.

ice cream dreams!
what does that mean?

nightmares all night. crazy dreams too. i think it was the brownie batter. u may or may not have made an appearance in them...

I laugh, my finger hovering over the screen. My skin warms when I remember his arms wrapped around me last night.

tell me about them later?
are u asking me out?:)
a phone call, jackass.

I giggle as I pull on shorts and a tank top. After I put on my makeup and calm down my hair, I pick up my phone again. There's a new text.

fine. but you have to call me.

Fair enough.

The pancakes are melt-in-your-mouth good. I mean, even-better-than-the-diner good.

Danny scoots around on the chair, smiling as he shovels his breakfast into his mouth. I grab a stack of napkins and place them next to him.

"Thanks Jazzy!" When he slides into my arm to nuzzle my hand, I go warm and gooey inside, just like this maple syrup. Maybe last night's mistake won't permanently scar him after all.

Mom looks between us, an anxious light in her eyes. She's trying.

Fine.

"Thanks for the breakfast, Mom. It's really good." I mean it, too.

"You're welcome." She pushes the pancakes around on her plate with her fork.

"It's so good!" Danny says. "I want to have pancakes every day. Can I have pancakes for lunch too?"

"You have a sandwich today," I answer. "Like every day."

"Okay. Can we have pancakes for dinner? Or for snack?"

Mom laughs. "We'll see."

"That reminds me," I say. "Today I'm going to Frankie's after school to get ready for my interview. You'll be home for Danny?"

"Sure." She smooths her hand along the table and doesn't look at me. "I'm going to do it this time, Jazz."

Her words are way too heartfelt for this early in the morning and the shock of it is like a chair being pulled out from under me. Trying to figure out how to respond, I take a deep breath, causing a mouthful of pancakes to go directly down the wrong pipe. I choke and sputter, managing finally, eventually, to nod and smile. I look at Danny, happily eating and rolling a toy car back and forth, and back to my mom. I hope like I've never hoped for anything that she means it this time.

"Jazzy, do you want to play UNO before school? I want a rematch!"

"Can't, bud. I'm broadcasting this morning. Remember I told you I have that important meeting next week? I have to get ready for it."

"Fine. But you owe me a game. No, you owe me ten games. I'll beat you all ten!"

I laugh and ruffle his hair. "You're on. But I'll be the winner. I'm onto you and your cheating ways!"

Danny narrows his eyes, little fist waving, but he smiles when I kiss his head.

"What interview do you have?" Mom asks, swirling the syrup on her plate with the fork.

I sigh. I've only told her about the internship a million times. She never listens. But I'm not going to argue again. If she wants to pretend we're a normal family, I will go along with it. Who knows, enough playacting and it may even come true.

"The WYN60 Get Up and Go morning show. Ms. Hudson has some good contacts there and if I can get an internship, along with all the stuff I do for the station at school, it would look really good on my college applications. I'm hoping for a scholarship."

"Oh. That sounds good…" Mom trails off, looking out the window again.

Why is she so strange? God.

"Yep. I'm excited." I rinse my plate in the sink. "But I have to get to school and get everything ready for my morning segment. You can tune in if you want. Today, I mean, or anytime really. It's 1620 AM."

"Oh yeah? I'd like that. Hold on, let me write the station down."

"Can I hear too?" Danny asks. "I never get to hear Jazzy on the radio."

"You're already at school when I'm on," I answer. "But maybe we'll find a way to record it sometime, okay?"

"Fine." Danny pouts. "But we're going to play UNO tonight, right? It will be a tournament. And no cheating. I mean, I don't cheat but you can't—"

Danny's speech cuts off suddenly and I spin around. His head is turned as if he's listening to something. I run to his side and squat in front of him, checking his eyes.

"Danny!"

He blinks rapidly. "What's wrong, Jazzy?"

My eyes cut to Mom. "Was it me or did something—" I stop, clamping my lips together. He doesn't need any more worry.

She nods sharply.

"Danny, do you feel okay?" I try to keep my voice as calm as possible.

157

"Yeah, duh! Gotta get my backpack!" He dashes out of the room.

"What was that?"

Mom shakes her head. "I'm not sure, but it didn't look right, did it?"

"I'm worried," I say. "It looked like he was going to go into one of his partials. Maybe he should stay home?" But I know as well as anything that we can't keep him home for every almost-seizure. He's missed enough school for the real ones. "I guess he has to go. Maybe I shouldn't go to Frankie's today. I can re-schedule."

"It will be fine." Mom's eyes lock on mine. "I'll be here. I promise."

Worry swirls in me but I decide to try to believe her. To try and trust. I kiss Danny goodbye and leave for school. Unease follows me like a storm cloud, but I figure I have all day to de-cide about going to Frankie's.

EVERY TIME MY phone rings or the intercom goes off, I jump in my seat, sure there's some horrible update about Danny having a seizure. By the time the final bell rings, I'm starting to believe he really is okay, at least for today. Maybe this morning was a fluke. He got distracted. Maybe it had nothing at all to do with his epi-lepsy.

When the final bell rings, I head to the radio room to get my backpack, which I forgot there this morning. I text Frankie to let her know I'll be a few minutes late meeting her outside.

Sebastian is coming down the back hallway. Ugh. Just what I need.

I give him a nod and try to scoot past him without stopping to talk. Fat chance.

"Jasmine!" He is way more overexcited to see me than he has been in a really long time.

"I'm kind of in a rush. Can it wait?"

"Not really."

I glance at my phone. Frankie's waiting. "Fine. I have like two minutes. What?"

Sebastian's eyes soften, his dark brows drawing together. "I miss you, Jasmine. Why can't you forgive me?"

I contemplate. "I forgive you. Happy?"

His eyes light up, hope filling his face with that look that turns his features from hard and severe to soft and innocent. Boyish. It's the look that always made me feel special, like it was reserved just for me.

"But," I say. "We're still over."

His face falls again. "But I was always there for you. With your family. Your brother. We were good together. I made a mistake. Why can't you accept my apology?"

I roll my eyes. "You were there for me, and I appreciate that. But when you weren't with me, you were with someone else."

"Are you perfect? Do you never make mistakes?"

"Not like that, I don't. And it was such a mistake that you changed your online status to single, like, the second we broke up? Yeah, I can tell you were so heartbroken."

"That's not my fault! Alexa changed it, I swear."

"Alexa changed it? Really, Seb? That's the best you've got?"

"It's true! She had been begging me to break up with you, but I didn't want to. I loved you so much. I do love you!"

"*Had been* begging? Had been? How long had she been begging Sebastian? Just how long exactly had it been going on?"

All the details I'd been questioning to myself, all the scenarios I'd imagined. Maybe it's even worse than I thought.

Sebastian goes hospital-sheet white at his slip up.

"It's over," I say. "I don't even want to know the details. I'm past this Sebastian, I'm moving on, and I'm finding happiness in my life now. I refuse to go backwards. I want to surround myself with people who are worthy of my time. You are no longer on that list. Sadly, I'm not sure you ever deserved to be. So go back to *Alexa*. Does she know how hard you're trying to win me back? Is she plan B? Or did you really think you could play us both again?"

His face falls in defeat. "It's not like that."

I pat him on the arm. "It's been real. Bye."

I walk away as smoothly as I can, even as the hurt tries to tug the scars on my heart open.

By the time I get outside, I find Frankie walking on the curbs like they're balance beams, arms out, tightrope-style.

"Took you long enough!" She calls across the lot, pushing the button to unlock her Jetta. "What's wrong? Is it the DJ Big Dee thing?"

My heart drops. "What DJ Big Dee thing?"

Frankie looks into the tree branches above me and rearranges her bangs. "Oh… Nothing. So what's wrong?"

"No. What did you mean by that? What's up with DJ Big Dee?" My stomach swirls into a tornado, bile creeping up my throat. I look over the top of Frankie's car. Her face crumples as if she's in pain.

"I heard a rumor. But it could totally be fake. I mean, I didn't hear it myself or anything."

"What was it?"

Frankie lets out a big breath. "She announced on her show this morning, supposedly. That she's a finalist for the Get Up and Go internship."

"Great. Just great."

I could throw up.

"I'm sorry. But whatever. They haven't met you yet! You will blow her away. Come on, let's go. Anyway, what's wrong? What was that sad look you had when you came out of school?"

"Sebastian," I say as I drop into the front seat of her car. I picture DJ Dee walking into the WYN60 building every day. Ugh. I shake my head to clear the image.

"No he didn't," she says. "What did he want?"

"I miss you," I say in a mocking voice. "We were good together. Forgive me."

"And you said?"

"Screw off? More or less."

Frankie pats my knee. "Atta girl."

I call Mom on the way, who assures me Danny is home and had his medicine and seems totally like his normal self. Frankie pulls into her driveway less than five minutes later. We raid the kitchen first and after settling on a bag of spicy Doritos and a huge bottle of water, we head to Frankie's room. Frankie's mom does a lot of work at their church and the whole family volunteers at tons of events, so she has lots of cute but professional looking dresses and stuff.

I try to ignore the sick feeling about DJ Big Dee and my conversation with Sebastian as I try on pretty much everything in Frankie's closet. I end up with a really pretty purple sheath dress that makes Frankie squeal and clap and almost fall off her bed.

"Perfect, perfect, perfect!"

I spin around in front of her full length mirror. I admit it does make me feel pretty confident. "Maybe this dress will be my lucky charm."

"You don't need a lucky charm!"

I put a hand on my stomach and look at myself from the side. "You sure I don't look fat?"

Frankie rolls her eyes. "You, fat? You're crazy!"

"I ate my weight in ice cream last night."

"After the fight?"

I'd filled her in about the fight with Mom during first period, but hadn't gotten to the details yet about meeting Wes at the park.

"I may have met up with a certain new friend who happened to bring me lots of ice cream to cheer me up?" I watch in the mirror as my face turns about three shades of red. Behind me, Frankie's mouth drops open. I pull the dress over my head quickly and pretend to be completely occupied with changing back into my clothes.

"Whoa, whoa, whoa! That is not the face of a girl who is only friends with a boy." Frankie rolls onto her back and kicks her legs in the air like she's riding a bike. "Oh my God, I want details."

I pull my shirt over my head and smooth a hand over my hair. I grin, knowing I can tease her a little bit more. "I really should get home."

Frankie jumps off her bed and scoops my flips flops up in her hand. "The hell you're leaving."

I drop down on the edge of her bed. I know better than anyone that a determined Frankie is unstoppable.

"Fine." I cross my arms. "What do you want to know?"

Frankie raises her dark, perfectly sculpted eyebrows. "I want to know whatever that little smile of yours is dying to tell me."

"What smile?"

"Nuh uh," she says. "Don't even try to deny it. Best friends, remember? Now spill."

I take a deep breath before launching into the story of Wes. I fill her in about all the stuff I haven't told her yet. It's not like I was exactly hiding things from her, because I normally tell her everything. I just didn't want to make a big deal out of stuff with Wes yet. But getting it all out now sends little flutters through me. When I finish the tale of last night's ice cream cheer up, she smiles.

"He sounds great," she says.

"He *is* kinda great. That's what scares me."

"What are you guys doing this weekend?"

"No idea." I motion to her to hand me my shoes. "I'm going to take it slow, though. I don't know if I'm ready for more guy drama."

"Why drama? Who says there would be any with Wes? If you ask me, that little smile says you're more than ready for Jasmine and Wes to be a thing. I think you like him. Like *really* like him."

I roll my eyes. "Come on, give me my shoes. If you don't mind, I need to get home. Just because Mom made pancakes doesn't mean she's going to make dinner."

"Right."

"What?" I laugh.

Frankie snatches her keys and follows me out of her room. "I'm onto you, Torres."

"Glad to know nothing has changed, then." I'm still laughing when we get into her car.

18

THE NEEDLE SCRATCHES on the record.

Stepping into the kitchen, the sound is unmistakable. I close the back door behind me. Frankie beeps as she pulls away.

I crash.

The high of the afternoon with Frankie, of last night with Wes…

I hear that stupid needle scratching and see Mom passed out and I just feel like someone has punched me in the face, kicked me in the stomach.

Dropping my backpack by the door, I trudge across the room. After I turn off the record player, I toss the empty bottle of vodka in the garbage.

What did I expect? I'm an idiot, a completely gullible idiot for expecting anything to change.

I go to wake my brother from his afternoon nap. His homework folder is on the kitchen table, his worksheets already complete. Huh. I guess she did something right today.

Whatever.

"Hey Danny," I say as I knock on his door.

His bed is rumpled and empty, but his feet poke out from his closet alcove, where he usually sets up and plays with his action figures. He slumps over the lot of them, snoring softly. Okay, this is definitely not a normal place to fall asleep. I sink to the floor and watch his steady breathing, wondering. Hoping he didn't have a seizure.

Danny sleeps a lot. His medicine makes him super tired. But he almost always naps in his bed or even sometimes on the couch. He doesn't usually fall asleep while playing with his toys, and certainly never sitting in his closet.

Of course there's no way to know what happened. And no way to know what he was doing or for how long. And considering things seemed off with him this morning...

I should have never gone to Frankie's.

I pick Danny up. Everything feels normal. Not the limp after-seizure effects. He opens his eyes.

"Hey!" I whisper. "What happened? You fall asleep while playing superheroes?"

He squints at me and looks around his room. He rubs his eyes. "Mom was going to do action figures with me. But I was doing them alone and then I was really tired. We did my math first. Homework sucks. It makes me sleepy."

"Don't say sucks," I say. The sick feeling in the pit of my stomach spreads further, making my limbs feel heavy and exhausted. Something about this feels wrong. "Come on, let's make grilled cheese?"

Danny follows me into the kitchen. I watch him carefully, but he seems okay. He doesn't even glance toward Mom on the couch. Amazing how normal this all is for him.

"Want to eat outside?" I ask. I don't want to look at her while we eat. So many emotions are warring in me, the strongest one of all being hurt. I don't even have any anger left. I just don't get it. How she can keep doing this and not care? How she can keep putting Danny in such serious danger by not being alert and aware?

I'm running out of options to keep my brother safe.

Danny takes paper plates and a bag of chips outside. He fills water glasses for us and carries napkins.

"Such a big helper!" I say. "I'll be out in like five minutes with the sandwiches. Go ahead and do swings for a few minutes, okay?"

Danny bounds back outside and I watch him through the window. I slip my phone out of my pocket and call his neurologist. They patch me through to the on call doctor and I explain what I saw with him this morning and then what may have happened tonight. Because of the medication changes, they agree he should come in, at least for a quick, in-office EEG.

Mom is going to flip about the cost, but I make the appointment for the next afternoon. She'll be at work anyway. I'll have to find someone to give us a ride.

Danny and I eat dinner on the deck and play more games of UNO than I can count. Mom is still asleep in the same exact position on the couch when I tuck him into his bed that night.

19

"GOD, I'D LOVE to slap Elena. Hard." Frankie seethes the next morning during chem lab.

"Yep. Me too. She was all apologetic this morning, of course. Remorseful, I'm going to change, blah blah blah. I didn't even respond. I'm so done with her lies."

"I feel awful I can't drive you and Danny though. I promised my mom I'd be at the senior citizen social this afternoon. I can't back out either or I totally would."

I nod. It's understandable. Church functions and volunteering take up a lot of Frankie's spare time, and she really likes doing that stuff with her family, which is cool.

Family. How do I get a normal one of those?

"It's fine. I'll figure it out. By the way, did you happen to catch the morning show?"

"Yeah, you were completely awesome. I didn't even know you were upset until I saw you. You didn't give any emotions away. You're totally a pro, Jazz. No doubt."

Happiness swells in my chest, despite how tired and upset I am today. I really hope she's right. A few more days and we'll see if I have what it takes to work at a real station. I stare out the window, daydreaming about going into the city every day. I can see myself, rushing around the broadcast room, helping and contributing to Get Up and Go, riding the train by myself into the huge city as if I belong there. If I get this internship, I will belong there.

Mr. Karns calls me over. I grab my lab pages before I go and pretend like I'm actually a functioning member of Easton High School.

WES MEETS ME at my house right after school.

"I totally owe you huge," I say as I climb into his car. I buckle Danny into his booster seat in the back. This has the potential to be really weird, bringing my little brother along, booster seat and all. But Wes doesn't bat an eye.

"I will think of a way to collect on that debt." He smiles deviously at me and I roll my eyes.

"You really have no shame do you? Even in a situation like this."

"Aw come on. I'm kidding. Trying to lighten the mood is all. And all's well with him, I'm sure."

His optimism buoys me almost as much as the comfort and familiar scent of his car, pine air freshener and that powder-sweet laundry detergent, which reminds me of our hug the other night.

Anyway.

"I actually owe you," he says. "My mom was making me go to this stupid college fair thing after school. I couldn't get out of it for anything until you called. Then *voilà*, like magic, she's fine with me missing it to come help you."

"Well, you're welcome too then," I say.

"What's up, little man?" Wes looks at Danny in his rearview. Danny is super excited about riding in Wes's car and bouncing all over the place in his seat.

"Nothing! I like your car! It's really nice! Are you my sister's boyfriend now? Hey Jazzy, what happened to Sebastian? He was your boyfriend, too."

"Whoa, Dan," I break in. "Calm down a bit back there, bud."
I give Wes a look that means to smooth over my brother's out-
burst, despite the fact that I'm mortified enough to crawl under
my seat right now.

Wes laughs as he changes lanes. "So, Danny. Your sister tells
me you like superheroes. Who are your favorites? I have a huge
collection of comics. I should show you them sometime."

"Whoa! Really?"

"Yeah, so who do you like? Are you a Marvel or a DC guy?"

"Marvel! Of course. Iron Man is the best! Who likes DC better, anyway?"

"I do have a thing for Batman," Wes says thoughtfully. "But
mostly, yeah, Marvel is definitely better."

"A thing for Batman?" I snort.

Wes's eyes cut to me. "Hey there. Watch it. No disrespecting
The Caped Crusader."

"Oh. My. God. Dork alert."

DANNY PLAYS WITH the toys in Dr. Bee's waiting room. I watch
him carefully, as if through a microscope. Nothing seems too off
about him, neurologically speaking, but after the two episodes
yesterday, my nerves are stacked like a delicate house of cards.
He dumps out a box puzzle on the waiting room floor and walks
circles around the pieces, trying to decide where to start.

"Jazzy, look! It's superheroes!"

"Very cool." My breath is deep and shaky as I watch him. I
just want him to be okay. Cringing, I text Mom to tell her where
we are. I get ready for an onslaught of yelling. I didn't tell her
this morning, because I didn't want her to tell me to cancel because of money.

"So yeah," Wes says beside me. "Your radio show was kind of awesome this morning. Not going to lie though, I was a *little* disappointed there was no dedication to me."

"And what would that dedication be?" I laugh.

"How should I know? You're the DJ!"

I give him a small smile. "Thanks for driving us," I say quietly. "I'm sure this is the last place you feel like being."

"It's not so bad."

"Whoa!" Danny yells, moving to the other side of the puzzle. "I think this puzzle has a hundred pieces!"

"See how many you can get before it's your turn with the doctor," I answer.

Danny happily goes back to his puzzle, shimmying from one end to the other as he puts the pieces together. He seems completely like himself, I decide, my worry trying to settle. On the television behind him, the news blares about wildfires on the West Coast.

Wes reaches over and takes my hand, cupping my fingers. Not threading them with his or squeezing them or anything, but cupping them, as if we're holding something delicate and precious in the space between our palms. I look down at them, every fiber and nerve in my body hyper aware. Sitting back in my seat, I tip my head back and close my eyes, leaving my hand in his.

IT TURNS OUT having Wes there is pretty amazing. Danny always has a hard time sitting still when they attach all the electrodes to his head and an even harder time waiting for the one hour test to pass. Wes distracts him by naming each wire on his head for a letter of the alphabet and then searching for superheroes or villains that start with that letter. I've never seen Danny so engaged and behaved during an EEG. When the technician turns the lights off and puts a movie on the television for Danny to lie still and watch for the remainder of the test, Wes sits next to me in the small testing room. He takes my hand again.

"Thank you," I whisper before putting my head on his shoulder and turning toward the television and the opening scenes of Disney's *Aladdin*.

What I wouldn't give for three wishes of my own.

Dr. Bee comes in shortly after the tech is done removing the nodes and cleaning Danny up.

She smiles and asks me for a recap on what happened at home to prompt today's visit, listening thoughtfully as I tell her. She looks Danny over and tests a few of his vitals before turning to me to talk. I ask if we can step into the hall to discuss the rest. Danny has enough to worry about, especially after overhearing Mom and I argue the other night. He doesn't need to hear about this stuff.

"Today's test looks okay," she says once we're in the hall. "There's still a lot of abnormalities, but it's the way his EEGs normally look. Nothing looks worse, certainly."

You have to love a trip to the neurologist. Abnormal brain activity that doesn't look worse is actually good news. Relief washes over me.

"So that's good, then?"

"As good as it gets right now," she says. "The new medicine is doing its job. Keep an eye on him, but also try to relax a bit too. He's in good hands and on good medicine. You know, Jasmine, you're taking a lot on yourself and it's really difficult for some people, even some adults, to handle. Where is your mom in all this?"

My stomach folds in on itself, the moment worse than a radio interview gone bad.

"She does what she can," I say. Then, because I am a minor and I don't want anyone to report us or something, I put on a big smile. "My mom works a lot, so I help out when I can. She's a single mother, so she has to work hard to support us financially. So I don't mind helping out with Danny whenever she needs a hand, even though she hates to miss appointments and stuff."

The lies roll out of my mouth one after the other. Yuck.

Dr. Bee narrows her eyes and hands me a pamphlet. "Check out some of these web sites. They have good resources for caregivers. We also have a once-a-month support group at the hospital, too."

She opens the door and walks back into the testing room. Danny and Wes lean over Wes's phone, reading what looks like a graphic novel eBook.

"Mr. McEnroe?" Dr. Bee says. "I didn't realize that was you."

"Hey Doc."

She smiles at me and looks between us. "I'm glad you have a friend to help, Jasmine. And Danny?"

My brother looks up at her, eyes flicking down to Wes's screen more than paying attention to her.

"You did awesome today. So I'll see you in a few months? Keep up the good work and have a great summer!"

Danny bounds through the waiting room, holding Wes's hand. "Can I see some of your comics today?"

"I don't know about today, but soon. Ask your sister when I can come over again."

"Miss Torres?" The receptionist calls as we're leaving the office.

"Hang on, Danny. Can you wait on that bench?"

Wes walks back to the little window with me, his hand on the small of my back.

The woman's eyes bounce between Wes and me. "Miss Torres? I ran your copay through the payment on file, but it wasn't sufficient for today's visit. You owe us forty-five dollars for today."

"Oh. Um. I don't have the money on me. Mom usually puts it on her debit card."

She turns a paper toward me. "Is that this card with the end numbers 7245?"

"I think so."

She lowers her voice. "The card was declined. I can take cash, check or another card."

This is so not happening right now. I look around the crowded waiting room and cringe. In the hallway, Danny races up and down the tiles, sneakers screeching.

"Can you bill us?" I whisper.

"I'm afraid not. We have to collect the copay today. The rest of the charges for your coinsurance for the test will be billed."

"Here, I got it." Beside me, Wes pulls out his wallet.

"No. You are so not paying for this."

"It's no problem."

I take a deep breath and contemplate the open wallet in Wes's hand, the receptionist's expectant look and Danny, still running up and down the hall.

"Jazzy!" he calls, an irritated whine starting to creep into his voice. "What's taking so long?"

The receptionist's eyebrows raise with impatience.

I really don't have a choice. I watch as Wes hands over cash to the receptionist, wincing when she gives him the receipt.

"You didn't have to," I whisper as we walk away from the window. "Anyway, I'll pay you back."

"It's no problem, really," he says. "You can pay me back if you really want, but you don't have to. Unless it's in kisses." He wiggles his eyebrows, trying to distract me, but I feel like total crap. I'm such a loser. A loser with a mom that sucks.

He bumps his shoulder into mine. "Knock it off. Where's your sunny smile?"

I roll my eyes. "You are so corny. And inappropriate. But thank you."

"That's what friends are for." Wes holds the door open for me. Up ahead, Danny hits the elevator button, pressing his full weight into it like he has some kind of elevator calling super-power or something.

"Yes!" I say to Wes. "Friends. So you finally admit the limits of our relationship."

Wes shrugs, a grin starting to turn the corners of his mouth up. "I can play along as well as you can. And anyway, I got you smiling again, didn't I?"

20

WITH THE INTERVIEW only a few days away, Ms. Hudson sets aside an afternoon to go over everything with me. When I get to her office, she has a plate of cookies and cups of tea for us.

"Are you ready?" she asks with a smile, her white flowery headband accentuating her dark eye makeup.

"Completely," I say. It almost seems silly, the amount of work we're putting into me getting an internship that will have nothing to do with actually being on the radio, but you have to look like a serious candidate if you want to compete. As Ms. Hudson has always told me, a foot in the door is a foot in the door.

We listen to all my recordings, cutting and splicing the best segments together. I nibble on the chocolate chip cookies and drink my herbal tea, watching Ms. Hudson work on my submission package.

"The woman you're meeting with is an old friend of mine and she knows you're my star radio student. I have a good feeling about this. Try not to worry, you'll do great. You're a natural on the air, so think of the interview like that."

"From your lips to the radio gods' ears."

We spend the next half hour going over things so I can be as ready as I can for Monday's trip. By the time we're done, I feel like I can do it. I say as much to Ms. Hudson and she laughs, her curly hair bouncing with the movement.

"Of course you can," she says. "Remember, you already *are* doing it. Now, I only have one tiny bit of advice left."

"Sure, anything."

"Make sure to have a calm and relaxing weekend. That will help you be on your game on Monday. Any weekend plans?"

I smile to myself, wondering what Wes has planned for us tomorrow night. "Not much. Laying low."

Not sure what my face says, but Ms. Hudson can obviously see through me. "If you say so," she says with a smile.

I giggle when I feel my face warm. "It should be a good weekend," I say.

It's enough to make her not ask questions but as I pack up and leave her office and start my walk home, I realize I really mean it. I'm looking forward to tomorrow night way more than I expected I would be.

Fine, I expected it. But still.

21

MOM WORKS A double Saturday so our paths don't really cross. She comes home shortly before Wes picks me up, but since I'm in my room getting ready, I can pretty much ignore her. Which is the way I like it. She wasn't happy with me taking Danny for the EEG, but whatever. He needed it and anyway, we have insurance. She can work the rest out. She's lucky I'm taking care of him, the least she can do is figure out how to pay for it. I still haven't forgiven her for that drunken night after her promise. I just can't be duped into believing things are going to change. I've noticed she hasn't been drinking the last two days, but I refuse to let the hope get any further than the tiniest shadow of a thought.

Hope is a strange and stupid thing sometimes.

I text Wes and tell him to call when he gets here. I don't want him coming to the door and God forbid meeting Mom.

I take one last look in the mirror and stuff my lip gloss and phone into a small purse. Wes told me to dress comfortably and in something easy to move around in. Whatever that means. So I'm wearing denim shorts and a casual top. I smile at the yellow shirt. So yeah, the whole *sunny* thing is really corny. But it's cute too and I'd be lying if I said I wasn't fishing for it.

Wes texts me not even five minutes later. I'm out the door with a quick kiss to Danny and a wave to Mom. I don't wait for her response. If I don't talk to her, she doesn't exist. Hence, no bad mood or bad date juju.

Wes leans against the passenger side door. He's wearing khaki shorts and a dark green tee shirt and brown braided flip flops. The setting sun highlights the natural blond streaks in the flop of hair that lies on his forehead. He pushes it back in that simple motion of his and gives me that smile smirk smile. Wow. Calm down, flailing stomach.

"Sunny," he says, pushing off the car, that wide, perfect grin stretched across his face. "You look amazing."

Blood rushes to my face and I look down at my sandals. "Thanks. You too."

"Come on," he says, throwing an arm across my shoulders and opening my door. This time I let him.

When he slides into the driver's seat he tosses me his iPod. "Here, you control the music. You know how comical mine can be. Besides, you're a DJ and all."

I giggle. "Okay, cool. But I need to know the theme of the night."

"I was supposed to theme it? Shit. I worked hard enough to come up with fun stuff to do."

"No, but when I do the morning show, there's always a theme to the day and the music revolves around that. Hello, I thought you've been listening to my show?"

His mouth quirks up in an adorably confused expression. "I have, but… I don't get it?"

"Okay, fine." I scroll through his playlists. "Can you at least tell me where we're going?"

"Of course. First stop, train station."

"Wait, what?"

"Second stop, Times Square."

I can't help it, I squeal. "Oh my God, really? New York is one of my favoritest places."

Wes looks proud of himself as he turns out of my neighborhood. I tap the screen and play some dance music. Something with a lot of bass. My heart thuds to the pulse of the music and excitement knots in my stomach. He turns up the volume as we drive toward the city.

FIRST OF ALL, who knew there was a massive and awesome laser tag center in Times Square? Apparently Wes did.

We run around the huge, dark rooms, lit only by neon artwork and black lights, chasing and shooting each other with laser guns. I think I land shots on Wes more than he lands them on me, but we're not really keeping score.

I'm at one of the reload stations, my gun locked into the machine that "charges" it with laser. I look over my shoulder, ducking out of view while in my vulnerable and unarmed position. The contraption lights up, telling me I'm ready to go, and I move quickly to get back onto the pseudo battlefield. When I turn, laser gun in hand, Wes is right in front of me, aiming at the canvas target on my vest. The laser lights up the target and he laughs like a maniac as I try to duck and weave around him.

We race into the next room, which is just as dark with plenty of shadowed hiding spots. I crouch behind a tower and wait. Catching him unaware when he turns the corner, I jump out and shoot the back of his vest, laughing as I run away. Eventually, our guns stop working, signaling the end of our paid time. We return our lasers and vests and walk into the bright lobby, wincing at the light.

Wes hands me a huge bottle of water and I take a big gulp.

"That was amazing." I nod toward the high tech battlefield, my adrenaline still rushing.

Wes smiles, cheeks flushed and with that flop of hair disheveled and pointing in different directions. "I've never been here. But laser tag used to be one of my favorite things in the world when I was a kid. It's gotten way more high tech since then. That was awesome! You hungry?"

My stomach groans in response and I grin. "Yeah. I think I worked up an appetite."

We press together as we make our way through the crowded streets. Wes wraps an arm around my waist to guide me. I lean into him, craning my neck to take in the skyscrapers and the animated ads on each building we pass, as high as I can see. The subway rumbles beneath our feet as we pass over the grates, the warm air rushing against our legs. We pass street vendor after street vendor selling souvenirs and artwork. Some of them sell food too, and the smell of roasted nuts and souvlaki meat adds to the intoxicating energy and sensory overload of New York. I bask in it.

"What are you thinking about?" Wes asks as he pulls a door open to usher me into a pizza place.

"New York," I say. "The energy is crazy awesome here. I'll be back on Monday for my interview. I can't imagine actually getting to be a part of all this every day."

Wes moves toward the dining room in the back, holding my hand to pull me through the crowd.

"You'll get it," he says definitively as he holds up two fingers to the hostess across the aisle.

I shrug as she seats us and push away all thoughts of the competition. "I really, really hope so. This is all I've ever wanted to do."

"You want to practice on me?" Wes asks as he opens my menu for me.

"Nah. I'm ready. I'm not even thinking about it until Ms. Hudson and I get on that train on Monday morning."

"You getting pizza or pasta?"

I frown at the menu. "I don't eat gluten, so I'm not sure I'm getting anything."

"What!" Wes's face drops. "Why didn't you tell me? Let's go somewhere else." He stands halfway and by the time I grab his hand I'm laughing loud enough to draw the attention of people around us.

"Got you!" I say, still laughing.

"You are pure evil."

"Come on. That was a good one. You totally fell for it."

He holds the menu in front of his face and doesn't answer. I walk my fingers across the table and hook them under his menu and wave.

"Seriously, though." I say, even though I'm still giggling. "This is the best night ever."

When he finally drops his menu, a pouty frown takes over his face. Reluctantly, he reaches across the table and takes both of my hands in his. I wiggle them as if to escape, playing like I'll pull them away. He tightens his grasp.

"It's not over yet," he says.

"I can already tell you," I say. "The whole night, all of it, is awesome. Even the parts that haven't happened yet."

Wes's eyes soften, even his smirk disappearing as his smile widens bigger than I've ever seen it.

I guess the laser tag made us hungrier than we realized because we order appetizers, salads and pasta and even though the portions are gigantic, I can't help myself—I eat every bite.

"Thanks for dinner." I hook my arm through his as we step back onto the busy sidewalk.

"Of course," he says, steering me down a side street. We walk that way through the warm night, arm in arm, for what feels like both five minutes and five hours, talking about everything under the glittering New York lights.

"Ah, we're here!" Wes stops in front of what looks like an innocuous glass doorway. I look up and see a huge vertical sign that says MIDTOWN COMICS and drop my face into my hands.

"Oh God, I can't get away from comics, even outside my house!" But I laugh as we push through the door and up a narrow staircase. Once inside, I follow Wes around as he explains various comic book characters and comic book styles to me. I'm clueless to most of what he talks about, but his excitement over it is pretty adorable. He buys a few things and after we check out, hands me a bag.

"A few for Danny," he says. "Some Iron Man ones that aren't so easy to find."

"That's his favorite!" My stomach starts to do that swirly acrobatic backflip thing again.

"I remember," he said. "A true comic fan never forgets another man's favorite."

This time when I hook my arm through his, I press a little bit tighter than I did before.

"Our final stop," he says a few minutes later, waving his hand with a flourish. My eyes widen when I look up and into the big glass window.

"Junction Records?" I clap my hands and rush through the door, Wes right behind me. While most people would probably lose themselves in the records and CDs first, I scan the store and head upstairs where I can see the equipment area. I pick up set after set of headphones and play with the sound boards. Even though some of this stuff is for performance DJs who mix records and get people on the dance floor, there is *some* overlap with the stuff I've always wanted to try out.

I slip on a pair of yellow Bortan headphones. They are the best of the best in the radio business. They're also crazy expensive. I close my eyes and press them against my ears. They feel like a million bucks. I imagine this is what some girls feel like when they wear diamonds.

A poster on the back wall of the section catches my eye. It's Brian, Sarah, Johnny and Latisha of the Get Up and Go Morning Show, endorsing the Bortan brand. Seeing their faces invigorates me. I run my hand along the poster. I am going to be in the same room as these people in less than 48 hours! I put the headphones back and grab Wes's hand, dragging him toward the records. We wander around a bit more, along with tons of other New Yorkers and tourists shopping in the famous store.

By the time we get back to Penn Station, I'm soaring on the high of the evening. We walk through the tiled hallways, his arm around me with my head on his shoulder. It's crowded when we get to the platform and Wes stands behind me, wrapping his arms around my waist. I lean back against him and he rests his chin on the top of my head, his fingers drumming softly against my stomach.

"Best night ever," I whisper on a shuddery breath.

We fill the train ride with nonstop talking and joking, but once we reach the car, we're quiet for almost the whole drive. I steal glances at Wes and contemplate things. If someone had told me I'd be breaking up with my boyfriend of almost a year and then finding this other guy, an amazing guy, really, I would've never believed it. I've always been completely against the rebound thing. I don't want to like Wes as much as I do already, but somehow, he's wiggled his way into my life. He's gotten under my skin. He's not only adorably cute and sweet and nice, but he's understanding too. He gets my family, and he's so great to Danny. I've even told him more about Mom than I have almost anyone except for Frankie. And he's nothing like Sebastian was. I feel deep in my bones that Wes would be trustworthy. That he *is* trustworthy. Wes is different than other boys.

But so much about him scares me, too. I could still get hurt. Bad things happen, no matter how nice someone is.

He's not Sebastian, Jasmine.

Or he could get hurt himself, get sick again. What if he did, start having seizures again, and I couldn't be there for him the way he would need me to? Because of Danny and Mom and everything else?

And yet... I really like him a lot.

Wes glances over at me. "Someone is deep in thought."

I smile at him, hoping my thoughts aren't obvious. "Just tired," I lie. "Tonight was amazing."

"So you've said." He pulls off our exit and stops at a red light. When he turns to me, his expression makes me all warm-gooey-brownie-not-quite-cooked-all-the-way-through inside. He traces circles on the back of my hand. "I'm glad you had fun."

"Me too." I close my eyes with my head against the seat and try to quiet the should-I-shouldn't-I voices is my head.

Wes pulls up at my house way before I'm ready to end our night. When he opens my car door, the warm breeze blows my hair around my face.

"Don't come to the door," I say. "My luck, my beast of a mother will hear us and come out to meet you."

Wes laughs, his hands fidgeting near his pockets. Nervousness suits him even better than his normal cocky joking act. I could almost throw my restraint out the window and lean into him for a kiss. It would be like stepping into the broadcast room without a plan for the day's show. Risky, but sure to work out. But I can't bring myself to do it. I obviously like him a lot and it obviously goes both ways. But even still. Not yet.

I fall against him, wrapping my arms tightly around his waist. "Thank you so much for tonight." My words are muffled against his chest.

I look up at him and smile. His lips turn up and his eyes study mine for a moment that seems suspended, as if everything else in the world has stopped. I lick my lips and he licks his and wow, only an inch forward for either of us and it would be all over. I can imagine that kissing him would be gentle and sweet and that

I could lose myself in it faster than you could say 'good morning listeners.'

He bends, ever so slightly. It's probably not even perceptible to a normal person, but to obsessive, analyzing old me, I watch the centimeters between us like the secrets of the universe are lingering there, just waiting to get pressed between us.

I raise onto my tiptoes, turning my head slightly so his lips land on my cheek. I squeeze against him tightly.

"Thank you so much, Wes. Tonight was simply perfect."

I take a step back. Wes swallows hard, his Adam's apple bobbing. He takes the hint, and there is no joking about kissing tonight, which somehow makes me feel worse. I walk toward my house, turning once more to look at him. I could still do it, could launch myself at him and bring my mouth to his.

Instead, I hold up the comic store bag and swing it in my hands. "Thanks for this too. It's totally going to make Danny's weekend."

Wes nods, brushing that flip of hair back and tucking his hands into his pockets with a faint smile as he turns to walk back to his car.

"You already made mine," I whisper.

22

SOMETIMES YOU WAKE up all groggy and cranky and like nothing is going right with life. But other times, it's the exact opposite of that, like life is a Disney cartoon and you live in one of those princess lands with singing birds and stuff.

Hello, listeners. Please disregard my pre-coffee, post-date, and obviously insane mental broadcast.

I shake my head to snap out of it and reach for my phone.

And smile when I see a text from Wes.

good morning sunshine

My response is a sunshine and smile Emoji as I flop back on my bed, reliving the night, detail by detail.

I probably should have kissed him.

Picking up the phone again, I giggle as my fingers tap the screen.

last night was so fun. Still in shock you didn't kiss me...
WHAT

I roll on my side and laugh, thinking how best to respond when he texts me again.

please tell me you're kidding
just saying. u didn't even try...

Silence for a good three minutes. I sit on the edge of my bed, staring at the screen and waiting for his response.

not the kind of guy who thinks you owe him after a night out.

omg I so was not implying that

My heart beats faster. I would never think that. Does he think I would think that?

haha he writes. **im joking. don't worry. i'll harass u for a kiss next time I see u, then. what are my chances?**

I put my phone on my nightstand and stretch. That was a mean trick. I thought he was serious. I grin. Just for that, he can wait for an answer. I yawn, noticing for the first time, the too-warm light streaming through my sheer curtains. I glance at the clock. After eleven! I have to get up. Tomorrow is the interview and I have to get everything ready.

"Hey sleepyhead!" Mom says when I walk into the kitchen.

Sleepyhead? Really?

"Did Danny have his meds?"

"He did. And we had pancakes. I saved you some." She pushes a few buttons on the microwave to heat them up. I fall into a chair with a thud. I'll play along with her act. But my guard is up higher than it's ever been.

I have to admit breakfast is delicious, though. Mom even sits at the table with me, offering me more as soon as I eat the first three pancakes on my plate.

"Thanks," I say. "They're really good."

"Thank you." She twirls the plate in front of her, round and round, while I cut the pancakes on my own plate. "So, how has school been?"

"Pretty good."

"Almost over."

"Yep."

This conversation is torture.

Outside, the bounce bounce bounce of Danny playing basketball in the yard fills the gaps in our awkward conversation. Must escape from this room. Like now.

"By the way," I say. "Ms. Hudson said you have to re-sign the permission slip for tomorrow. I missed the trip last time but since we are going on a different day and taking the train instead of a bus, I need permission."

"Sure!"

She's trying way too hard, smiling all clownish big and everything. I have to legitimately force my eyes not to roll.

"Do you need something new to wear?"

"Nah. I borrowed something from Frankie."

"Cool."

"Yep."

"So did you have a nice time last night with Sebastian?"

"Mom. Really? Sebastian and I broke up."

"I'm sorry. I didn't know. So who were you with?"

"A friend."

I'm being meaner than I need to be. I realize that. She's only asking simple questions. But despite my floating on clouds wake-up this morning and the pancake effort, I'm still not ready to be that generous with my forgiveness.

I finish my breakfast and wash the dish. Mom still sits there, staring at me, like we're going to continue this awkward heart to heart for the rest of the day.

"So… I'm going to go get my stuff together for tomorrow."

"Oh… yeah. Okay. Let me know if I can help."

"Thanks. I got it."

I escape to my room and drop into my desk chair. I guess I could have been nicer. She was trying. And sober. I reach for my phone and laugh out loud when I read Wes's text.

hello? i am dying in suspense here! my chances? what are they? ;)

I SPEND THE rest of the day prepping for tomorrow. Ironing the dress, practicing my makeup and gathering all the materials for my portfolio and resume. Ms. Hudson calls me in the evening to go over the details for the morning schedule and by the time I have to turn on the lamp in my room against the waning daylight, I feel one hundred percent, completely prepared.

I'm so happy that I decide to eat dinner and watch a movie with Mom and Danny. Mom orders pizza. Okay, so it's not cooking, but still, it does require some effort on her part, and she only drinks water as far as I can tell. She even lets Danny stay up a little late, since the school year is almost over, and she lets us both pick a movie. He picks *Dumbo*, I pick *Frozen*. Mom even sings along to a few of the songs and I'm surprised by how nice her voice sounds.

I tuck Danny into bed just after ten o'clock and come back into the living room to help Mom straighten up.

"Thanks for tonight," she says. Her eyes search mine and I can see what she isn't saying out loud. *I'm trying, Jasmine. I really am.*

Well, I'm trying, too.

"It was really fun, Mom." And then, because I feel like I owe her something else. "Seriously. Let's make it a weekly thing, maybe? Danny was so happy."

"And you?" She looks down at her hands.

"Me? Yeah. It was cool."

Mom wipes down the counters in the kitchen and hums under her breath.

My chest heaves a little, seeing her act like a normal mom. Between tonight and last night, it's like I'm living in a parallel universe. Let's hope tomorrow completes the trifecta of things going well.

My English textbook waits for me on my nightstand. I'm too excited about tomorrow to sleep, but Mr. James assigned some short stories that looked boring enough to do the trick.

I flip my air conditioner on and slip into bed. Just as I suspected, the first story has me half asleep by the time I turn the page. As I'm reaching up to turn off the lamp, there's a knock on my door.

"Come in."

Mom stands there, holding a small wrapped box and wearing a very goofy smile. I sit up, confused. If she bought me a gift, this really is taking the whole new her way too far.

"A boy just came by," she says, her smile growing even goofier. "A very not Sebastian boy, I may add."

He didn't.

"He said to give you this but to wait five minutes so he was sure he was far enough away that you couldn't come out and catch him. He's funny. And cute. Very cute."

I roll my eyes and hold out my hand for the package.

"So is this the not Sebastian you were out with last night?"

"I assume it must have been. Blondish hair?"

She nods.

"That's Wes. He's cool. A good friend."

She raises her eyebrows and gives me a small smile.

As soon as she's gone, I tear off the wrapping paper.

Oh my God!

He bought me a pair of Bortons! Oh my God! I rip the plastic package open and pull out the headphones. They're yellow, exactly like the pair I tried on last night. I can't believe this. This is crazy. Too much. Wow. I've always wanted a pair of these.

I grab my phone.

"Wes!" I screech when he answers. "What did you do? Oh my God, thank you, this is crazy. Wow."

"It's a good luck present," he answers, all nonchalantly too.

"This is insane, Wes. These things are super expensive."

"It's nothing. I wanted to get you something to wish you luck. Not that you need it."

"I'm… I'm actually speechless right now."

"First time for everything. But seriously, when I saw your face when you tried them on, I had to."

"How did you get them?"

"At the mall. Junction Records isn't the only place that sells them. Didn't take all that much research to find out where else I could get them."

Wow. He did all that for me? So… incredibly thoughtful.

"I'm totally going to wear these next time I broadcast. You should come by the Easton station one morning to hang out while I do the show. Before school."

"I'd love that."

I slide the headphones over my ears. "Seriously, I feel all professional in these. Hang on." I hold my phone out to take a picture with them on and send it to him.

"Just sent you a pic." I say. "Don't mind my no makeup and pajamas."

"Is it something revealing?"

I snort. "I'm ignoring that one. But seriously, best good luck present ever. I am definitely going to be showing up tomorrow feeling like a legit, real, professional DJ."

We chat for a few minutes before hanging up. I lay the Bortons on my nightstand and turn off the light. I don't sleep for a while, thoughts of tomorrow's trip, Wes, and Mom all rolling around in my brain, begging to be figured out.

Sometimes when things feel too good to be true, you have to just roll with it.

23

NEW YORK CITY field trip to WYN60 Get Up and Go. Take two.

This time me and Mom are up at the crack of dawn. She makes me eggs, and while I'm eating she gets Danny up, gives him his medicine and gets his stuff ready for school.

Twilight Zone, indeed.

I meet Ms. Hudson at school and we take her car to the train station. She's her normal self, barely even talking about the interview, but I'm practically crawling the train car walls with nerves. It's already been narrowed down to a handful of final choices, one of which I know is DJ Big Dee, who I already wasn't able to beat the one time when we faced off in a live competition. Plus, who knows who else is in the running that may be even better than her.

"Jasmine," Ms. Hudson says sternly, smoothing out her white floral dress. "Relax. You'll do great. Internships are not so demanding. They will listen to your stuff and know you have a future in radio. Believe me, *they* would be lucky to get *you* for the summer!"

As soon as we exit Penn Station, excitement courses through me, the city thrumming with the bustle I love. It's hard not to think back to Saturday night, being here with Wes. I smile to myself, the memory of his hug warmer than the June sun overhead.

Ms. Hudson leads the way, pulling the door open to a very tall and impressive looking skyscraper. As soon as the elevator opens on the thirty-seventh floor, The WYN60 logo is bigger than life and my excitement skyrockets. This is really happening, isn't it? I expect everyone to be much older and smarter than me, probably wearing business suits and fancy hairstyles and in general being way cooler than me. I'm filled with a sudden fear that they'll look down on me and think I'm just a dumb kid.

The receptionist sitting at the front desk is trendy in the way I've always imagined most native New Yorkers tend to be without even trying, with her cropped asymmetrical haircut and a drapey silver shirt and red leather pants.

"Welcome to WYN60!" Her face brightens when we walk into the reception area. "Do you have an appointment?"

The Get Up and Go show is being piped in throughout the speakers and I listen closely, hardly believing that I'm in the building where it's being broadcasted. Like, live, as in right now.

We're shown into an office and Ms. Hudson and I wait in matching leather chairs opposite a big glass-top desk. On the walls are all kinds of pictures of various celebrities and radio personalities. Award trophies and plaques line one shelf and framed gold and silver records line another.

Ms. Hudson winks. "You got this," she mouths.

A few minutes later, a woman about Ms. Hudson's age walks in. She's impressive, tall and stylish in a smart black suit. She's absolutely beautiful and the way she carries herself, straight back and poised, with complete confidence, shows how professional she is. She gives Ms. Hudson a hug, reminding me that the two women are old friends. My phone vibrates in my bag and I look quickly between them, hoping neither of them heard it. I kick it under my chair, saying a quick, silent prayer that everything is okay and that buzz wasn't about Danny.

"You must be Jasmine," she says, shaking my hand firmly. "I have heard so very much about you. I'm Roberta Jackson."

"Thanks for seeing us today," I say, crossing my legs and making sure to sit up straight. "I've been working in our school radio station since freshman year, and it's the only thing I want to do with my future. Just being in this building is more excitement than I've ever had, I think."

Her smile grows even wider and she takes a sip from a glass of water. "I'll tell you what," she says. "I know you have your samples and recordings, which of course I want to hear. But why don't I give you a quick tour of the studio and office? We can even get a peek in on the morning show, if you want?"

If I wasn't sitting down, I think I would probably faint. "That sounds great." I keep my voice as calm and professional as I can. "As long as you're sure you have time. I know you're very busy. I don't want to take up too much of your morning."

"Nonsense." She stands up. "Follow me. You can leave all your things here."

I walk beside her as we make our way through the halls. She points out various departments: marketing, art directors, sales, and accounting. It's all cubicles and so many people I can hardly take it in. Plus, she's walking and talking quickly, so I don't have much time to stop and notice much.

We walk down a long hall, with a tiled floor and low, warm lighting. Like most places in the office, this hallway is lined with pictures of Brian, Sarah, Johnny and Latisha of the Get Up and Go show, standing and sitting with various pop stars and other celebrities. I have the urge to touch the pictures, their faces. A fleeting feeling grips me, a dream really, one I don't even want to allow myself… imagining my own face on these walls someday.

Hello, New York City, this is Jasmine Torres with Get Up and Go, wishing you an awesome Monday morning.

Holy goosebumps.

"And here, of course, is the broadcast area." Ms. Jackson walks quickly, her heels clicking like a metronome on the floor.

"How many years have you been here now?" Ms. Hudson asks.

"Me? Thirty-four years. Can you even imagine? We were kids back then, weren't we?"

Ms. Hudson smiles.

Ms. Jackson looks at me. "Your teacher and I went to NYU together and interned here forever ago. After a few years in the business she was the smart one to get out to make a difference. And here I am, still here." She waves her hands as if to say she's stuck here, but it's obviously not true. Not that Ms. Hudson doesn't love her life, because she chose to leave radio for teaching. But come on, Ms. Jackson runs one of the most successful radio stations in New York City. I doubt she really regrets her decision to stay. How could she?

I gape at the ON AIR sign above our heads. I'm heady with the excitement of being here. Please, please, please let me get this internship. Even if I'm walking through these halls for long shifts and doing nothing but making copies or picking up lunch, it will be a dream come true.

Ms. Jackson pushes a door open and we enter the studio. There's a glass window separating us from the broadcast area. I try not to gawk as I watch the DJs. The four of them sit around the table, computer screens and microphones in front of each one, bulky headphones resting on their ears. They interact seamlessly, volleying conversation around the table as if they're a family having dinner.

So unbelievably cool.

"And behind us," Ms. Jackson is saying. "These are the sound engineers and producers." I turn around and wave to the few guys at computers in the room with us.

"This is amazing," I say, feeling like a cartoon character with stars swirling out of my eyes.

"Thanks," she says. "We're proud of our little family here. Come on, let's head back."

Little family. Wow. She really is modest.

I walk next to Ms. Jackson on the way back to her office. Ms. Hudson hangs back, letting us talk. When we get back to the office, Ms. Jackson goes over my resume and listens to the clips we brought from the last few weeks of morning shows.

"Your interview skills are solid." She nods as she backs the recording up to hear another segment again. After a few minutes, she looks at me and smiles. "You obviously have the knack and hard work ethic for radio. Your themed segments are really great, and as you can see, listeners respond well to you."

"Thanks," I answer coolly. Coolly! As if I wasn't just complimented by one of the most powerful women in radio in one of the leading radio cities in the world.

About that trifecta of stuff going well? Yeah. Life is good.

"So you know this internship doesn't allow any on air time, right? I'm sure Ms. Hudson has explained that to you? Our college interns are a little more involved in the recording room than the high school interns, but even those are not on the air."

"Yeah, er, yes. She has. I know I'd be working in a supportive role to everyone here at WYN60. I'm more than happy to do whatever you and everyone else here needs."

I don't say what I'm really thinking, that I'd lick the dirt off her shoes for a job here.

She nods. "At this point, we have the candidates narrowed down to four finalists."

Four others? Gulp. I begin to deflate.

"You understand this is a very competitive business and many, many high school students applied for this one spot."

"Yes, I can imagine how many applicants you had to screen." I try to keep the warble from my voice.

"We had more than two thousand applicants for the high school intern spot."

Double gulp.

"Your clips are very good and as I said, you have some very solid skills. The other applicants, however, are also very talented."

Fully deflated now. I knew I didn't have a chance. Who did I think I was fooling?

Of course the other applicants are very talented. Way more than me, I'm sure. I probably only got this interview because of Ms. Hudson, anyway. My clips are probably one of the worst Ms. Jackson has ever heard, but she feels obligated to say nice things to me.

I clear my throat to bite back my embarrassment.

She sits back in her chair, holding my transcripts and resume up again. "Any idea where you'll be applying to schools next year?"

"None yet. But I've been compiling a list of schools with good communications programs."

Again I don't say what I'm really thinking. I'm compiling a list of schools I can't afford and hoping for a miracle to land in my lap.

"As well you should." She smiles and drops the papers on her desk and hits a button on her phone. "Mark?" she calls into the speaker.

"Yes, Roberta?" A friendly voice answers.

"Can you bring me a welcome kit, please?"

A welcome kit.

A welcome kit!

Wait.

I don't even want to think it. That can't have anything to do with me. Can it? It can't be *for* me? I mean, it obviously, *has* to be. But it can't be.

"Give me two minutes," Mark answers.

Roberta presses a button and looks up at me with a smile. "Welcome to WYN60, Ms. Torres. We are looking forward to having you on board as one of our summer interns."

My cool mask of fake composure slips. "Oh my God! I mean, thank you so much!" I can feel the tears pooling in my eyes.

Great Jasmine; nice way to hang on to that air of professionalism.

But Ms. Jackson is smiling and when her assistant, Mark comes into the room, she passes the Get up and Go tote bag to me.

"Welcome," she says. "Once again. Mark, this is Jasmine Torres, one of our new summer interns. Can you ask H.R. to bring over the paperwork? She can bring it home and fill it out with her parents over the weekend."

"Hey Jasmine!" Mark, a pudgy guy with glasses and a cool style, wearing a bolero hat and striped vest, gives me a small wave. "I'll get that paperwork right over."

And then Mark is gone, and Ms. Jackson and Ms. Hudson are reminiscing about college and I just sit here, holding a bag chock full of goodies like tee shirts and notepads and pens from my absolute favorite radio show and station which happens to be (gasp!) the new place I work.

What is life?

We leave about twenty minutes later, with the human resources (which is apparently what H.R. stands for) paperwork. Ms. Jackson shakes my hand when we leave and I take a look around the WYN60 office, knowing (and hardly believing!) this will be my new surroundings three days each week this summer.

I'll even earn a small stipend—enough pay for my commute and lunches and hopefully some left over to help out at home.

As soon as we get out onto the sidewalk, I squeal, jumping up and down.

Ms. Hudson high-fives me. She slides her sunglasses on, but not before I notice tears in her eyes. "I'm so proud of you!" She says. "You didn't even need me here. That was a home run, Jasmine, from the minute you walked in the door."

I bite my lip. "It was, wasn't it? I was in some kind of weird robot mode. I didn't want to look like a dork, but I was so excited!"

"You worked so hard for this. It's well deserved." She squeezes my arm. "Now let's get some lunch."

We choose a small café with sidewalk seating. We look over the menu and I decide on a veggie burger and sweet potato fries. All the energy expended on this morning's meeting has left me exhausted and absolutely starving.

"I'm going to text my friend and tell him what happened," I say, slipping my phone from my bag.

"Friend?" Ms. Hudson asks, a small smile playing on her lips.

I shrug and laugh. "It's complicated."

Two missed calls from Wes? That's weird. He knows where I am today. And a voicemail? I press the phone to my ear, confused.

"Hi Jasmine, this is Lynette, Wesley's mom. There's been an accident. I know he would want me to call you."

She pauses, her breath hitching, and my stomach drops like I'm doing a freefall right off the side of the earth.

When she speaks again, her words are muddied with tears. "We're at St. Bonaventure. Room 356 in ICU. I wanted to let you know. You meant a lot to Wes. *Mean* a lot, I mean. I know he'd want me to tell you."

The message clicks off and she's gone.

"What's wrong?" Ms. Hudson's voice shows only a fraction of the alarm I feel. "Is it your brother?"

I shake my head slowly, forcing words from sticking in the arid desert my mouth has become. "We have to go," I manage.

24

MY MOM ANSWERS on the third ring.

"Mom!"

"Jasmine, hi! How did it go?"

"What?" My mind darts all around. Frantic thoughts on top of frantic thoughts, chasing more frantic thoughts.

"The interview. How was it?"

"Oh. It was great. I got the internship, but—"

"Congratulations! I knew you could do it. We have to celebrate."

"No. Mom. That's not why I'm calling. Wes is in the hospital."

"Who?"

I huff. "Wes, Mom! My friend Wes. The boy from last night. With the Bortans. The headphones? The guy with the present!"

"Oh, him! Is he okay?"

"I don't know. His mom left a message for me. She said there was an accident. But she said he would want her to call. *Would want.* That doesn't sound good." A sob works its way out of me.

"Oh honey."

"Anyway, Ms. Hudson is going to drop me off at the hospital. Is that okay? Are you home for Danny after school?"

"Yeah, of course. Sure. Want me to come to the hospital?"

I squeeze my eyes shut and shake my head. "No, that's okay. But thanks. I'll call you when I know something."

THE INTENSIVE CARE floor is way quieter than pediatrics ever is, and when I get off the elevator the hush falls around me like the loudest thing ever. The waiting room is smaller, too, and has none of the fish tanks or toy centers that the pediatric floor has. It's tiny, really, with about ten ugly paisley chairs and three scarred up wood end tables. Wes's mom paces there, whispering into her cell phone, the lines on her face deeper than I remember. She wears cotton shorts and a tee shirt and no makeup.

I glance at the nurse's station and decide to wait for Lynette to end her call. I'm not sure if I'll even be allowed to see him, but if I don't at least find out soon what happened, I'm going to lose it. I take deep breaths and shove my shaking hands in my pockets as I pace the short hallway. It takes serious mental strength to keep my mind from landing on every bad memory of Danny's visits in this place.

Her words are too low for me to hear and her back is to me, but I watch as she reaches up to wipe tears away.

An accident? I don't even understand how that happened. He should have been at school today so what was he doing driving?

When she finally hangs up, she sees me and gives me a small smile. She crosses the room on big steps and pulls me into a tight hug.

"Thanks for coming, darlin'."

"Of course! What happened? Can I see him?"

She glances toward the hallway beyond the nurse's station. "He looks terrible, I don't want it to scare you. Let's go walk. We'll get a coffee real quick and talk for a few minutes."

"Okay." My heart is racing. I want to cry or scream or do something that makes her tell me what's going on, but of course I have to bite my lip and wait patiently. "He's okay, though. Right?" My voice goes up an octave and my eyes search hers.

She hooks her arm through mine and leads me toward the elevator. "I don't know," she says with a catch in her voice.

The elevator is crowded so it's not until we're in the coffee shop that Wes's mom opens up. I stir my drink and wince at the memory of when I met Wes over my spilled cup of hot coffee.

"He had a seizure this morning."

No.

I close my eyes and picture Wes's face. Perfectly healthy, seizure-free Wes.

She takes a deep breath, obviously gearing up for a story she's probably told a million times today. "He's been doing so well. You know, he hasn't had a seizure in years. Years! But this was a bad one. And he was at the top of the stairs. He fell all the way down and broke his nose, wrist and ankle. But he also hit his head very hard and has a concussion. Concussions are dangerous enough for healthy people, but for those with epilepsy, they can be detrimental, as can any change in the brain. Anyway, he was still seizing when I came home from the grocery store. They are trying to pinpoint the timeline now, but the cuts he got in the fall were already starting to congeal and scab and the way the fluid gathered at the breaks in his bones, suggests he was on the floor for quite some time, maybe even close to an hour."

"Oh my God." I stop walking.

She nods. "I know. And I wasn't gone much longer than that, so it must have happened right when I left."

"How is he now? Is he coherent?"

Tears spill down her cheeks as she shakes her head. "He is totally out. Heavily sedated. They used the diastat to stop the seizure, which worked for a while..." she shakes her head and takes a deep breath. "But when we got here he had another small seizure and then an hour later, another, a worse one. They gave him IV meds and upped them to the point of him being almost catatonic. They had to slow everything down in there." She taps her temple.

We step onto the elevator, which is thankfully empty.

"He has regular EEGs so we know his epilepsy hasn't been getting worse. I am praying this is a fluke breakthrough seizure and not his epilepsy getting bad again. Or something worse."

I close my eyes and lean back against the elevator wall. "Has he had an MRI?"

"Going in for it in an hour."

I exhale and think about the odds. Abnormalities in the brain, like growths and tumors, are common causes of seizures. But Wes already has epilepsy, so I'm hoping the odds of having both are slim. But still.

"I better get back in his room. A volunteer was sitting with him while I made calls and got coffee. But I need to be in there. Wes's father is flying home from a business trip. But he's in Asia, so it'll be quite a while yet until he gets here."

I swallow the now massive lump in my throat. "Let me come with you," I say. "I've been through this so many times with my brother. I know how hard it is to sit there alone, and besides, I really want to see him."

Wes's mom considers me for a minute and then nods. "Come on," she says. "Just be warned. He's pretty banged up."

She wasn't kidding.

Wes has a cast on his ankle and another on his wrist. Tape stretches across his nose and cheeks, his face swollen and bloated, his skin scraped and marred and tender-looking. He looks like a stranger. His eyes are closed, but bruised a deep, deep purple beneath them. My fingers tremble, wanting to touch his cheeks. Wanting to make him better. His head is covered with the electric EEG nodes and wires and cap of course. An IV needle is taped to his arm and two bags hang next to his bed. Wires snake beneath his shirt too, monitoring his heart. His arms are scraped up, as are his legs.

"Oh, Wes," I whisper. My breath catches in my chest like a wild bird beating its wings to escape. I watch the waves on the monitor that spits out information on what his brain is doing. Impossible for regular people to read, even after a million hospital visits watching those screens for some type of answer. Some type of small clue.

I drop into the chair next to his bed, his mom sitting on his other side. I scoot the chair closer and gently take his fingers in mine. I remember only last week when he cupped his hand over mine while I worried about Danny in Dr. Bee's waiting room. I stare at his face, trying not to wince at how mangled he is. I will him to open his eyes, to laugh and joke around with me.

Please be okay.

I'd been worried about Wes having seizures again. That I wouldn't be able to handle it, to deal with someone else in my life who suffered this way. But this sitting here and hoping he's going to be okay is worse. So much worse.

Just please, please be okay. Please don't let it be too late.

We sit there for hours. Watching his face, the monitors. Nothing changes. I wait in the room with Wes's mom when they take him for the MRI. They wheel his bed back in, but still nothing changes.

Mom calls me around ten. She's insistent I come home and I know she's right. As much as I'd love to sit at Wes's side all night, I know I can't. Lynette promises to call me as soon as there is any information or change. I leave with a promise to be back in the morning.

Mom picks me up with Danny asleep in the backseat. She smiles sadly and pulls me into an awkward hug across the console. She smells like peach shampoo and sugar, as if she was baking. I pull back and look at her. Her eyes are totally clear. She's sober.

I burst into tears and hug her again.

25

AFTER A RESTLESS night, I take my nervous energy into the kitchen before dawn, looking for something distracting. Everything is sparkling clean. Huh. The counter is even completely cleared off, not a bottle of anything in the way of my making breakfast. I look in the cabinets, in Mom's normal alcohol spots, and see nothing. It appears she has cleared out all the booze.

I pop an English muffin in the toaster and pace by the counter, sipping coffee. I nearly choke when I see Dad's old stereo sitting by the back door with the cord wrapped around it tightly. Wow.

I have no missed calls or texts, which means there was no change with Wes last night.

I text Frankie and tell her what's going on. I hate missing school yet again, especially considering I am almost at the allotted days off, but there's no way I'm not going to the hospital as soon as I can.

I mean I have to, right? Bile creeps up my throat, picturing Wes in that hospital bed. I'm sure he'll be okay. But he looked so...

I take a deep breath and grip the edge of the counter. The cheap Formica digs into my palms. My reflection stares back at me in the window over the sink. It's muted, the green grass and pebbly walkway drowning out my face as if I'm a faded watercolor painting.

What if I don't go? Wes's mom can update me, I'm sure. I mean, maybe I really shouldn't miss school again.

Or maybe I can't handle this.

I jump back from the sink, turning quickly away. My hands shake as I carry my breakfast to the table and sit. How could I think such a thing? I care about Wes. So much. I'm not a heartless, cruel person.

Am I?

I sit in the silence, nibbling on the cold English muffin while I stare at the blank white fridge door, studying the chips and dents in the surface, dents I've never even noticed.

I think about Wes. His silly dancing, our night in Times Square, his face in the comic shop as he explained his favorite superheroes, the way his smile quirked up as he watched me try on headphones at Junction Records, the dramatic way we fell into each other, breathless after laser tag. And of course the hug, that amazing hug. The way he brought me ice cream and how he sometimes joked about giving me a kiss. I squeeze my eyes shut, but the tears still manage to break through.

A barely there smile tugs at my lips. I really do care about him. But this is terrifying, and way too familiar.

Danny pads into the kitchen a few minutes later and I pull him into a fierce, tight hug. He steps back, eyes wide, and I try my best to wipe my emotion off my face.

"Time to get ready for school, Danny. It's your last week!"

"What's wrong with you? Why are you crying again?" He juts out his lower lip and my heart dips like one of those paper airplanes Wes is always flying.

"What? I'm sorry. My friend is sick so I was worried, but I'm happy, see?" I force a fake smile. Danny returns it tentatively.

"Waffles?" he asks.

"How about Cheerios," I say. "*After* you get dressed."

"Fine," he says. "But stop crying, Jazzy. I don't want you to be sad."

Once he's gone I mentally curse myself for my emotions worrying my brother. But I can't help it. I'm scared and upset, and I'm angry, too. Wes shouldn't have to go through this, and Danny either.

It's not fair.

And what else isn't fair is me stepping away. But I think I have to. Not all the way away or anything. Just a little distance. A little space. I'll go to school today. I'll check in with Wes's mom on the phone. Danny needs me more than anything. What if I can't be there for them both?

I already hate myself as I reach for my backpack.

26

WHEN I GET to the hospital, the same nurses are at the desk as when I left last night.

So fine. I didn't make it to school. Not even half a block from home, I turned around and went back to ask Mom for a ride to the hospital. The feeling that tried to keep me away, that inside out hole in the bottom of my stomach, pulses with familiar fear. But as I walk into the hospital, I know this is where I belong, and where I want to be. Being with Wes is worth any bit of worry that may come with it.

So I nod to the bottle blond nurse from last night, the cheerfulness of her pink puppy dog scrubs ridiculously out of place in intensive care. Her eyes light up with recognition when she sees me.

"Hi again," I say quietly when I step up to the desk.

"Hey there," she drawls with just a hint of a southern accent. "You were here for Wesley, right?"

I nod, grateful I don't have to wait for a pass. I scrawl my name in the visitor log and head down the hall toward Wes's room.

Lynette is in the hall just outside his room, looking down and scrolling through her phone. A cart of food trays is parked in front of her so she doesn't see me at first. She looks up, eyes weary and red rimmed. When she sees me, her face breaks into a smile.

"Jasmine."

"Any change?" I glance over her shoulder into the room and see Wes looking almost exactly how he did when I left last night, though from here, the bruises look even darker, maybe.

"The MRI was clear, thank God."

I let out a breath. Thank God, indeed.

"The EEG was looking a little better last night. So they are slowly decreasing the IV meds. He's still out of it, but I am really hoping he wakes up soon. It was a really long seizure, who knows what may have... I just want to look in his eyes and hear his voice and know he's okay in there, you know?"

Do I ever.

"Can I go in?"

"Sure. I'm running for breakfast while my husband is here. Come on in, I'll introduce you."

When I step into the room, the cool darkness invades my senses suddenly, like someone's thrown a blanket over the sun without warning. The shift is almost too much to handle after the bright morning outside and the fluorescent lights in the hall. A man sits on the other side of the bed. He's an older replica of Wes, sandy blond hair and all, except his has some snowy white in it. He smiles at us when we walk in, and it's uncanny how much his grin mirrors his son's. Even the way he shifts on the bed is eerie, leading his lean frame with his shoulders first. They carry themselves the same.

"Hey George, this is Jasmine, Wes's... friend."

Wes's dad walks around the bed to shake my hand. "Nice to finally meet you, Jasmine. Thanks for coming by."

"Of course. Where else would I be?" I try to ignore the traitorous twitch in my belly, reminding me that I almost didn't come. Because what I feel now completely trumps what I felt this morning. It's true: Where else would I be?

I look at the monitor across from Wes's bed and then let my gaze travel to him. Blinking quickly against my threatening tears,

I reach out and gently pat the sheet that covers his legs. *Come on Wes, wake up.*

When I look back up, Wes's parents are wearing matching soft expressions.

"I can see what Wes means," his dad says.

I cock my head, waiting for him to explain.

"Wes thinks very highly of you. I can see why." He threads his fingers with his wife's. "You know what, Lynn, let's go grab breakfast and let Jasmine visit with Wes."

"Yeah?" She leans against her husband, her face a little more hopeful when she looks up at him. I wonder again what it was like to grow up in Wes's house with nice parents who love each other and seem so normal.

"Talk to him," his dad says to me as they step into the hall. "Maybe it'll help."

When they leave, I pull up a chair beside his bed. Just like last night, I lace my fingers with the ones on his good hand.

"Wes," I say. "It's Jasmine. You have everyone pretty freaked out here. You're getting better though, so I'm sure you'll be awake any time now. Your parents are so nice. I got to meet your dad this morning and I hung out with your mom last night, too. Your dad said he's heard of me. Can you wake up so I can tease you about that? I want to know what you're telling them about me."

I watch the monitors, but of course, nothing changes.

"So, anyway. I got the internship yesterday. I start the first week of July and will work at WYN60 for three days a week, for eight weeks, until almost when school starts up again in the fall. It was amazing, being there. Everyone was so nice. I even got to see the broadcast room with the morning show on the air. It was awesome."

I walk over to the window and tilt the blinds open, just a little. "Let's let in some sunlight. It's nice out. Maybe it will help, if you can feel the sun. I wonder if your phone is around here. Maybe some of that heavy metal would be the perfect remedy to wake you up."

But Wes doesn't move. The soft skin under his eyes is so bruised and painful-looking. Black-blue rings circle his eyes and though some of the swelling has gone down, his nose is still so swollen he doesn't look like himself at all. My gaze travels the scarred map of his face, the cuts crusted over with scabs, layered on top of the near-black bruises.

"Oh, Wes." I reach out to touch him, careful as if he'll crumble beneath my fingers. My hands linger on his shoulder then move up to his cheek. "It will heal," I say, for my own benefit, maybe. He barely looks like the Wes I know. My Wes.

I let my fingers rest on the mesh cap that covers his scalp. The soft flop of hair I love peeks out from between the electrodes and I push it to the side and back as much as it will go. The way he always does.

Wes shifts on the bed. It's such a slight movement, I'm not sure it's real. My heart flutters and I trail my hand to his shoulder again.

"Wes?" I whisper. "Can you hear me? You're okay. I'm here. Me, Jasmine. And your parents are here, too."

Nothing.

The monitors show no change. One thing I've learned from being here with Danny, is that while it's nearly impossible to read anything on them, there will usually be a spike or some visible change on the charts with movements, even eating, blinking, or certainly, waking up.

Damn.

I lean closer to him, my gaze darting across his features. Are his lips parted more than they were a minute ago? Has something changed or contorted in his face? His eyelids flinch. If I wasn't so close and wasn't staring, I would have missed it.

213

I reach down and grasp his hand with mine.

"Come on Wes," I say. "Open your eyes. They're giving you less medicine now, and they said you'd wake up soon. Do it now, Wes. We all want to see you."

We want to know you're okay. That you're the same Wes you were.

More flutters. Blinking, even. He's waking up. Hope unfolds in me, crackling bits of excitement waking up in every one of my pores.

"Wes?" I say softly. "Hi Wes."

His eyes open and I raise up a little, my cheeks aching with how wide I'm smiling.

"Hey," I whisper.

He blinks a few times, confusion clouding his features.

"You're okay," I say, the nervous knot in my stomach twisting with hope that he really is, that there's no lasting damage. "You fell." I leave out the part about the seizure. Too much information may possibly be too much to handle. "How do you feel?"

Wes's eyes slowly come into focus. It's like magic, watching the emotions cross his expression, watching his features soften and warm when he recognizes me. Watching him come back to himself in there. To regular Wes, my Wes. My fingers twine tighter with those on his good hand.

"Sunny," he says, his lips curving into the slightest of smiles. "Why the hell does everything hurt so bad?"

A laughsob squeaks out of me and happy tears prick the corners of my eyes.

"You broke some bones," I say. "No dancing for you for a while, I think."

"Some? Feels like I got run over by a Mack truck. Jesus."

If he wasn't so hurt, I'd throw my arms around him in the tightest hug. But I lean down instead, carefully, softly, and press my lips to his. His warm and dry and perfect lips. It's only for a second or two, but when I open my eyes and pull back, he's smiling a little bigger, and in the depths of his bruised and swollen face, his eyes glitter with familiar mischief.

"I knew you'd kiss me." He shifts on the bed and winces at the pain. "And that you'd make the first move, too. Of course, I didn't think I'd have to go to these extreme measures for it."

I perch on the small strip of bed next to him, his hand still resting in mine. I reach for the call button next to his bed.

"We need to call the nurse," I say. "And your parents. They're getting food downstairs."

He lifts his hand to stop mine. "In a minute," he says. "How about another one of those kisses first?"

I laugh at Wes and shake my head. But I lean down again. What can I say? It's good to have him back. I push all the horrible things that could have happened from my mind as I press my lips to his, light as a butterfly landing, and pretend this moment is the only moment there is.

27

THEY KEEP WES in the hospital for only two more days. I visit as much as school and visiting hours will allow. His EEG has calmed down again, his medicine is adjusted and he is sent home with his parents. After school, I drive over to his house, trying not to gape at the sheer size of the place. I think our house could literally fit in his garage. I pull Mom's rusted old Honda into the driveway and dash up to the door.

Wes's mom answers with a smile that doesn't quite reach her eyes. Exhaustion has deepened the lines around her mouth and left heavy, dark circles beneath her eyes. "You don't have to knock, Jasmine. You're one of the family."

"Thank you, Mrs. McEnroe. It's nice to see you. Here, I mean. Instead of the hospital."

Her smile widens as she steps aside to let me in. A fancy crystal chandelier hangs in the two story foyer and I fidget, feeling out of place. This house is all echoey and stone and strangely empty feeling. It's like a museum. But she pulls me into a hug that manages to make me feel warm and at home, despite all that. I do belong here.

"It certainly is nice to be home and doing well," she says. "Wesley is right in the living room, watching TV. I'll bring you guys some snacks in a little while."

I turn toward the room, but she stops me with a hand on my arm. "Thank you, Jasmine, for being there for Wesley."

"Of course."

"I wanted to tell you how much he's changed since he's known you. It's not just how happy he is, either, though that *is* the best part."

My cheeks warm. What do I even say to that?

"But he acts different, too. Just before this all happened with the hospital, he broke down and admitted he wants a gap year before college. He said he's wanted it forever but couldn't get the nerve to tell us."

I swell with pride for Wes that he finally talked to his parents about this. "That's great that he—"

"It's because of you," she said. "Wesley said, if Jasmine can stand up and be honest with her mom, why can't I? I wasn't happy at first. I admit it was an adjustment. But, I want him to be able to open up to us and I don't think he ever realized that he can, that all we want is for him to be happy. So thank you, Jasmine, for your example to him."

"Oh. Yeah. Well… you're welcome."

"And thanks for caring so much about him," she whispers before walking away. "He is simply *crazy* about you."

I slip into the massive living room, where Wes lies on a leather sectional couch watching *Top Gun* on a huge widescreen TV. A guy wearing sweatpants and a tee shirt sits on the other side of the couch, feet up on an ottoman, and with his hat tipped back.

"Sunny!" With a wince, Wes drops his legs to the floor and pats the couch next to him.

"Hey," I look between the two guys.

"Oh yeah," Wes says. "This is my friend Jacob."

Jacob gives me a chin nod. "What's up?"

"Jacob was just leaving," Wes says.

"I was?" Jacob looks genuinely surprised. I remember the story Wes told me about how Jacob is an overgrown frat boy. I can totally see it.

"You were." Wes raises his eyebrows and Jacob stands and stretches.

"Fine, fine. I can take a hint."

"First time for everything," Wes mutters. Jacob fist bumps Wes and nods to me on his way out of the room. "Nice to meet you."

Once he's gone, I plop onto the couch. "Sorry to interrupt your guy time," I say.

Wes shakes his head. "You could never be an interruption. Jacob's been here all day. It's fine. How's the newest Get Up and Go intern, anyway?"

My face flushes but my smile's so wide my cheeks hurt. "Just fine, thank you."

"Come closer," he says. "Have I mentioned how proud I am of you?"

"Only about a zillion times at the hospital." I scoot closer to him and carefully rest my head on his shoulder. He drapes his good arm around me and pulls me closer.

"Well it's true," he whispers against my hair.

"Does this hurt?" I pull back, trying not to put too much of my weight against him.

"It's a good hurt," he says, pulling me closer again until I'm curled against his side.

"Seriously. How do you feel?" The bruises around his eyes are starting to fade into a puke yellow color and the swelling has gone down considerably. His shaggy hair hangs over his eyes and I reach up and push it back. Nice to see him without the EEG hat or wires. He looks almost like Wes again.

"Like I was beat to hell?" He snorts. "For real. This blows. Everything hurts."

"I'm so sorry. What did the doctor say when you left?"

"Everything will heal or whatever. Don't worry, I'll have my pretty face back soon."

"No. I mean Dr. Bee. Did you see her?"

"Yeah." His eyes cut back to the TV and he shrugs. "It is what it is."

"Wes."

"What? Shhh. This is the best part." He turns up the movie and the sound of fighter planes fills the room from the surround sound speakers.

I sit back against the couch and watch the dip and flight of planes on the screen, wincing at the shooting sounds. Once Goose's plane goes down, I gently take the remote from Wes's hand and turn the volume almost all the way down.

"Wes, come on. Talk to me."

He lets out a sigh and turns toward me. "It sucks, okay? I've gotten so used to being the guy with epilepsy who didn't have to deal with seizures. Seven years, you know? I don't want to have to worry about this crap again. Plus, now I can't even drive for six months. Sucks."

I don't want to have to worry about him either. Words stick in my throat. Anything I could or would say feels like a cliché right now.

"Anyway, doc thinks a med adjustment will do the trick since the seizures have been so well controlled for so long, but you know, with her normal caveat about how epilepsy is unpredictable..."

"That it can change and do what it wants without warning," I finish for him.

"Yep."

I swallow the worry, push it as far, far down as I can. I choose today to live in the moment. Worrying solves nothing.

"But it's all good," Wes says, threading his fingers with mine. "You know me. Once this heals," he motions to his face and body. "I'll be as irresistible and sexy as ever."

"Um, Wes?"

He tilts his head and looks at me, eyebrows raised in question.

"Not that you need me to feed your ego, but I have to throw you a bone here since you're so pathetic looking right now."

"Oh?" He licks his lips as his eyes lock on mine.

I stretch my body until my face is even with his. Leaning in, I give him a slow kiss, teasing his bottom lip with my teeth. "I think you're pretty irresistible right now."

My words vibrate against our mouths.

"Oh really?" He kisses the corner of my mouth. He kisses my jaw and just below my ear. My collarbone. His lips make a slow and gentle path along my skin until they reach my mouth again.

"Yeah, really." I say. "And sexy, too." My words are swallowed by his mouth as he traces my lips with his tongue. A soft moan escapes me and I press myself against him as he kisses me and kisses me and kisses me.

"Sorry," I say. "This has to hurt you."

"Hmmm." He shakes his head, the fingers on his good hand tangling in my hair as he pulls me impossibly closer. His lips are gentle and rough and soft and hard and new and familiar and a million other things I can't describe because my brain is exploding in nerve endings. His mouth finds mine over and over again with a rising sense of urgency as he pulls me tighter against him still. I've never been kissed like this. I didn't even know this type of kissing was possible.

When we come up for air, I fall back against the couch, chest heaving and body thrumming as I try to calm my breathing. Wes leans back against the plush cushions, and after a moment seems to collect his own breaths as a satisfied smile spreads across his face. He motions to his body and face again.

"I can't believe this is all I had to do to get you to make out with me."

I laugh and rest my head on his shoulder. All jokes aside, this is simply amazing. I'm still rocked by what happened to him, as he and his family are too. Seven years without a seizure and then a major one that really hurt him, and that could have been a lot worse. Luckily there doesn't seem to be any lasting damage in his brain, just the broken bones and scrapes. And the sense of safety and control ripped from him. From all of us.

"You think you'd be up for leaving the house in a few days?"

"Um, where to? I'm not really up for planning any big nights out, fun or horrible, but I can probably hobble somewhere close by."

"My school's end of year carnival. I kind of have to go, as I'm broadcasting the first hour from there. It will probably be mostly dumb, but there will be good food, and games and stuff. It's down at the community park so I could prop you up on a bench or something."

"Prop me up? Geez, you make me sound like a mop." Wes laughs, and it's that deep, honest, totally amused and happy laugh that I really, really love. He winces with the pain it causes, but his smile doesn't falter for long.

"Come here, you." He pulls me closer, dipping his head to kiss me again.

28

"GOOD AFTERNOON EASTON High! Welcome to the Hello Summer Carnival and I'd like to give a big, huge shout out to the student organizers and parent volunteers." I flip my headphones on, the gorgeous yellow Bortans from the sweetest boyfriend a girl could have. "I'm playing a summertime mix for you all, so mix, mingle, ride and eat, and mostly, sit back, relax, and kick off your summer with some fun in the sun!" I start my playlist and music screams from the speakers around the impromptu DJ table. Ms. Hudson gives me a thumbs up from over at one of the food stands. I wave back and scan the crowd for Frankie.

"Are you taking requests?" Wes hobbles closer to the table, his crutches clattering loudly.

"That depends," I answer, pushing my headphones down to hang around my neck.

"On?" Familiar mischief dances in his eyes. He licks his lips and I shiver, remembering the last few nights where hanging out at Wes's house and kissing was pretty much my one and only agenda. All in the name of nursing him back to health, of course.

"What's in it for me?"

Wes shakes his head and laughs. "All in good time, my Sunny. All in good time." He hobbles with his crutches, moving around the table. I slide my headphones back on to change the song. I'm dying to tell him about the surprise I have planned for him later today. I can barely contain it, like putting a cap on a container of lit fireworks.

"All right, Easton students and parents. Hope you're having fun out there. Here's a good one to pump up the blood and energy level around here. Feel free to dance if you're stuck in line. DJ Jasmine Torres highly recommends it." I hit a few buttons and push the headphones off again.

Hands grasp my waist and I jump, turning around quickly to see Wes's devilish grin.

"Holy crap," I say. "You scared me."

"I'm sorry," he says, bending his head to mine. "Make it up to you?"

I roll my eyes, but I'm at a loss for my normal sarcastic quips. What can I say, Wes's lips? They unarm me.

He gives me light, but sexy kisses, slow ones that press and pull back, teasing me even as I return them, making me hungry as hell for more. And he does give me more, but just a little at a time, the kisses coming one after another, slow and soft and steadily rising, like he's been gifted with some kind of insane and intense gift for buildup. Like I'm being kissed by someone other than an ordinary boy. I shiver against him.

A familiar voice behind me breaks the spell.

"Well, well, well." Frankie says. "I am assuming this is Wes. So is it true? Do I finally get to meet mystery boy?"

I spin around and smile at my best friend. "Indeed it is. Don't mind the bruises, though. He's normally very cute."

I giggle at my insult and he digs his fingers into my waist, making me jump and laugh harder.

"Yeah," he says to Frankie. "Don't mind them at all." He lowers his voice. "She's a bit rough when we… you know."

"Oh my God, Wes!" I smack him on the chest as the song is ending.

"Hang on," I say.

"Hello Easton. This is my last set coming up. It's been great serving you this year and playing the tunes that make you groove. I'm turning the mike over to DJ Romeo, so have a good summer!"

I bob my head as the last set starts and look out over the crowd. My school may be tiny and dumb at times, but it's my place. And I know I'm moving up next year to senior and to bigger things beyond. I'll be a New York City intern this summer at WYN60 and Get Up and Go. This school? This town? It's just the beginning for me.

Speaking of beginnings.

Frankie and Wes wait for me outside the DJ area, talking about who knows what. I pack up my equipment and hand the broadcast over to the next student DJ before hopping down from the platform.

"You kicked ass!" Frankie says, excited as always. "Now, let's get some cotton candy!"

Wes pulls me in for a hug and drops his lips to mine again. I kiss him back, taking care not to bump his broken nose.

"Great," Frankie says. "Is this what I have to watch all day?"

I laugh and pull away, feeling my cheeks warm. "Sorry," I say. But I can't help it. I snuggle into Wes's side once more and give him a quick peck on the cheek.

Frankie rolls her eyes. "Okay, enough already. You, get your equipment. You, get your crutches. This girl is starving."

I hike my bag onto my back. "Hang on," I say. "My mom and Danny are coming. I promised them I'd eat with them and introduce her to Wes."

"Wait, what?" Frankie steps back. "Elena is coming here?"

I nod and can feel the small smile playing on my lips. "Things are getting better. So much better. She has a really long way to go, but I think she means it this time. I hope she means it this time. She's even going to AA meetings or whatever." I lean in and lower my voice. "She even sold the stereo."

"Wow," Frankie says, hooking her arm through mine. "This shall be known as the year of transformations."

We walk slowly as Wes clomps along on his crutches.

"Speaking of, jerk at three o'clock."

I follow her gaze and see Sebastian at the Tilt-a-Whirl, his arms wrapped around yet another new girl.

"Is that Kelly DeMarco?" Frankie asks incredulously. "Wow, Seb gets around, huh?"

"I think it is," I say. "Good luck to her. Sebastian gets sick as anything on rides. He'll probably puke all over her."

I giggle as we walk in the other direction and I can honestly say, other than shock at seeing Sebastian at a school event, I no longer feel any emotion toward him at all. The lingering scars he left remain, but I am so much happier now.

I get funnel cake for me and a sausage and peppers sandwich for Wes. Frankie traipses off in search of cotton candy and I search the field behind the food vendors for signs of the surprise I've planned for Wes. My eyes light up when I find where they've set up the trailer.

"Cool," Wes says, looking up. "We have a good view from here."

I smile. "Of course. I planned it this way." But this isn't the half of it, I want to add, as the airshow begins, small planes doing dips and loops overhead. The crowd oohs and ahs, people plopping down on the grass and filling the tables around us to watch the show.

Frankie comes back with my mom and Danny in tow. "Look who I found!"

Danny bounds over to us. "Wes!" He throws himself at Wes, wrapping his arms around him.

Wes winces. "Hey kid, what's up?"

"Careful Danny, Wes has some broken bones," Mom says, coming up behind my brother, holding a tray with hot dogs and

French fries and drinks. Her daisy chain tattoo peeks out from under her watchband and I smile.

"Danny do you need me to cut that up for you?" I nod to his hot dog.

"I'm not a baby, Jazzy. You don't have to do stuff like that. I'm a big kid. I'm always trying to tell you that!"

"Oh. Yeah. Of course you can. Go for it." I scoot back on my seat next to Wes and he squeezes my hand. Danny's right, he is perfectly capable of doing things for himself. I've gotten so used to taking care of him, it's just become natural for me to worry all the time and do everything he needs. Kind of like Wes's mom did to him over the years. But Danny is growing up. And he needs some independence.

I scoot over to make room for Mom. She plops down beside me and starts divvying out the food. Her hands shake a little less today, her body still going through alcohol withdrawal. I hadn't realized what a physical dependency she had on the booze, only what it was doing to our family. I get it now, that her alcoholism is a disease, just like epilepsy is for Danny. I vow again what I told her last night, that I will help her when she needs it, that I'll try to be more understanding. I'll even go to the meetings or whatever if I can. She has a really long way to go, but she's trying and willing. I hope it sticks. For the first time, I really truly believe it could work.

She looks up at the sky and smiles at the airplanes. "This is really cool," she says.

I put my sunglasses on, blinking back a sudden and furious gathering of tears.

The airshow lasts about half an hour. Wes's grin is bigger than I've ever seen it, his eyes dancing with the movements of the planes. The excitement in my gut barely lets me enjoy the show. When it's over, I tap Wes's arm. "Come with me," I say. "I have a surprise for you."

He raises his eyebrows but hobbles up to standing.

"Have fun!" Frankie yells as we leave the table. Mom grins. I clued them in earlier.

"That was incredible! Wow. Did you see that prop plane? So cool. But, what's this surprise stuff about?" Wes asks, huffing as he crutches across the field. I had this idea before his accident, and was glad they could still accommodate him, crutches and casts and all.

"I told you I'd pay you back," I answer, weaving through the grounds slowly, with a hand on his arm.

"Really? Are we going back to my house or yours?"

"You really are such an idiot." I laugh.

We step onto the grassy area behind the last vendors and Wes's smirk falls from his face. He looks at me, wide-eyed, and once again, I can imagine exactly what he looked like as a little kid. That same magic lights his features now.

"What is this?" he asks.

The planes from the airshow are lined up on the field. "They're done for the carnival, but I got a few to stick around so you can tour them and check them out. I know you've always dreamed of the Air Force and being a pilot and have a thing for planes, so I thought you'd like it."

"Oh wow," he says, mesmerized by the planes.

"And," I say, barely able to contain myself. "They are going to take you up, too!"

"What?" Disbelief tinged with excitement turns Wes's features into an even more adorable canvas than usual.

"Yep. The parent who arranged the whole thing actually owns one of the planes. The Quest Turboprop, it's called?

"What! Are you serious? This is amazing!" Wes starts movin faster on his crutches, his eyes darting between the planes.

I grin, feeling as proud as if I'd built one of these planes m self. "Yep. He agreed to take you up for a low ride. I kn you're big on the old planes. The pilot says this is probably the closest to the kind you've always wanted to fly."

Wes shakes his head and looks out over the field, obviously drooling over the planes. "Jasmine, this is incredible."

I laugh. "I think that's the first time you've called me by my name."

Wes stares at the planes on the field. "Momentary insanity, Sunny."

"Come on," I say, moving toward them.

Wes bends down to kiss me, one hand cradling my cheek. His few soft kisses deepen quickly and border on getting a little too intense for a big, wide-open field where anyone can see us. He pulls away and rests his forehead against mine. Our breaths come quick between us.

"Thanks," Wes says. "For the dream come true."

I hook my arm through his, and help him cross the field.

Dream come true, indeed.

This is DJ Jasmine Torres, signing off. Have a good day, listeners. I know I will.

Acknowledgments

There is a book in every writer's life that is the "book of their heart," and *This Ordinary Life* is it for me. This book resonates on a deeply personal level and has been percolating for some time in my subconscious. Thank you to everyone who helped me take it from those deep recesses of my mind to these pages, to make it a real, live, breathing thing that I can hold in my hands. (Yes, books are living things!)

Thank you to everyone whose support and loving guidance helped to shape this story, specifically my beta readers and critique partners: your tough love was quite simply the one and only reason this book came to be. Thank you Kate Boorman, Erin Brambilla, Lauren Cerruto, Dawn Miller, Jamie Reed, Shveta Thakrar, Becky Yeager, and extra thanks to Melanie Kramer whose endless brainstorming, rereading, text messaging, chatting, and emailing helped make these characters who they have become.

Hive five to everyone in the YAWN crew, too! :)

To all my various writing groups: The LBs, The Purgies, the Ynots—thanks for being there as we all take this crazy journey together. (And becoming some of the greatest friends, in the process.)

To my editor Tracy Richardson and my publisher, Luminis Books. I'm so happy to work on another project with you all again!

To my family and friends, whose love and support of not only my writing, but also my life, keep me going. I could not exist without you.

To my parents for their endless, unwavering, support and pride: Thank you. I love you so much.

To my husband and children, who give me so much encouragement and help and endless understanding and support—I am so grateful. You put up with so much when I'm in novel-writing mode, and I thank you for not minding unfolded laundry or leftovers.

And to all those whose enthusiasm for my books keeps me writing and excited to share them with you: Thank you, a million times, thank you! I read every reader email, post, or tweet with a huge smile on my face and a heaping dose of gratitude in my heart. Thank you for reading my books and being excited about them. I am so lucky.

To everyone in the epilepsy community: we are in this together. Never stop fighting.

Thank you to everyone who picks up my little book. I hope you enjoy it!

About the Author

Award-winning author Jennifer Walkup is most often found writing, reading, and spending time with her husband and young sons. A member of SCBWI and RWA, Jennifer also works as an editor and creative writing instructor, and is an advocate for epilepsy awareness. *This Ordinary Life* is her second novel.

You can find her online at www.jenniferwalkup.com.